CATCH A RISING STAR

Laura Phillips

A KISMET˙ Romance

METEOR PUBLISHING CORPORATION
Bensalem, Pennsylvania

To Mom, who made gardens seem like special places.

LAURA PHILLIPS

Laura Phillips is a former reporter and news editor who began writing fiction after her first child was born. She lives in Kansas City, Missouri, with her husband, three children and assorted pets. When she isn't writing or doing Mommy jobs, she can be found in the backyard garden.

ONE

The pungent odor of crushed sage tickled Beth's nose, and she stifled a sneeze. Then she lifted the heavy pedestal in the center of what used to be a picture-perfect herb garden. Finally the pedestal was upright, with the brass sundial back in place on the top.

She sagged onto the ground, eyes closed, no longer caring whether she muddied her clothes or crushed a patch of tender herbs beneath her. Not that it mattered, since there was no one to see the stains except bugs, animals, and the hired hands. As for the herbs, most were already flattened. That black witch of a milk cow had trampled the carefully tended garden fairly well. It would be weeks before the sage recovered enough to be harvested for market. The basil and mints were still in good condition, though, and for that she was thankful.

For a moment, she lay there in the sun, letting the warm, earthy fragrances of moist earth and crushed herbs surround her and restore her peaceful frame of mind. But before she could fully relax, she heard a soft flutter of wings. Beth opened her eyes just as a glossy black crow landed on her leg.

"Go away, Edgar," she muttered. The bird repeated a garbled imitation of her order and dropped a shiny strand of silver on the ground nearby.

"What's this? My lost necklace," she exclaimed, half rising and stretching her fingers toward the necklace. But the crow snatched it up and flew away.

"Damn," she muttered, sinking back. For a moment she lay there, soaking up the sounds and smells of the farm and wondering how she would pry her necklace away from her pet. The crow had stolen it from her dresser a few days ago after it had slipped through a tear in the screen—a tear that was much larger now. She knew Edgar hid all sorts of shiny objects in the rotted crook of an ancient mulberry tree behind the house. However, she decided the necklace wasn't worth the risk of climbing twenty feet from the ground. Nothing was worth that.

Grimacing, she sat up and brushed a damp copper curl off her forehead, then tucked her hair back under the battered, broad-brimmed straw hat. It was hot there in the sun—humid, too, after this morning's heavy rain. Mother Nature must have gotten her dates mixed up, Beth decided, because this sultry mid-May afternoon felt more like July.

Slowly, she eased her tired limbs upright and got back to work. She spent the next hour filling in the cow's muddy footprints, trimming the damaged plants, and replacing the scattered mulch. She kept up a running conversation with Edgar, who returned minus the silver necklace. She was nearly finished when a honking horn caught her attention.

A scattering of trees blocked her view, but she could tell by the frantic honking that someone had a problem and that someone was on her property. Two hundred acres of pastureland and woods separated her produce gardens from the highway, and the sound seemed much closer than that.

Trowel in hand, she leaped over a row of rosemary bushes and trotted down the driveway, following the noise past the house and around the bend. Then she spotted the car and something else that sent her blood pressure soaring. Standing in the middle of the narrow wooden bridge at the foot of the hill was a big black cow, the same one that had wreaked havoc in the herb garden. A shiny blue sedan edged slowly across the bridge toward the cow, but she didn't move.

"Charley! The blasted cow is out again," Beth bellowed at the top of her lungs. The gray-haired, wrinkled gnome of a man was already ahead of her. He trotted out of the woods and scrambled jerkily under the fence. He held a coiled length of rope in one hand.

"The fence is down somewhere along the south end of the pasture," he explained between breaths. "She must have gotten out there."

Beth fell into step beside him. "If that idiot in the car would stay put and be quiet, we might be able to catch her on the bridge." She shot the old man a sharp glance. "If the fence is down, why did you put her in that field?"

"Didn't. One of the boys must have. Told 'em to put her in the north pasture till I fixed the fence in the south field. Must've gotten mixed up."

"It figures," she answered. "Damn. That noise is going to spook her into the hayfield."

Charley cleared his throat. "That's your mother's new car. Brought it out last week to show you, but you were gone. Guess I forgot to mention it."

Beth frowned. "If that's Marlene, we're in trouble."

Charley bobbed his head in agreement. "Fool woman never did have any sense about animals. Never could figure out how come she's so—"

"Different," Beth interrupted, then lengthened her step to a distance-eating lope that left Charley behind. A moment later, she decided she needn't have hurried. The cow faced the car impassively, holding her ground. As Beth neared the bridge, she slowed and eyed the cow warily. With a quick slicing motion of her hand, Beth signaled her mother to stop. Stop pushing the cow with her bumper. Stop honking. Stop everything.

Glancing over her shoulder, she noted that Charley wasn't so far behind her after all. Already his singsong crooning, his way of gentling the crazy black witch into submission, worked its magic spell. Grinning, Beth watched the cow prick up her ears and swing her body around. Then the cow bellowed disdainfully and relieved herself on the bridge. Beth stopped altogether and wrinkled her nose in disgust.

Never breaking rhythm, Charley winked at Beth as he passed. Moving more slowly now, he approached the cow and slipped an arm around her neck. Within seconds, she was firmly caught with the rope and following Charley up the road. Noting Charley's tired shuffle, Beth took the rope from him.

"You ride," she said. "Come on, Witch, out of the road." While the old man climbed into the backseat of the car, she tugged the cow off into the grass and waved to her mother. For the first time, she noticed that Marlene hadn't come alone.

Eyes widening in surprise, Beth took a step toward the car. Marlene had never brought anyone to the farm before, not even Alfred. When she'd married the wealthy businessman five years ago, she'd escaped the hand-to-mouth existence she'd endured for forty years. And she didn't understand why Beth chose to move back to the run-down farmhouse forty miles from nowhere, not when a private suite awaited her in the penthouse on the Country Club Plaza. Marlene didn't understand, either, that Beth preferred farmhands, old ladies, and animals to the glittering company her mother kept these days.

Before Beth could get a good look at the shadowy figure behind the tinted glass, a tug on the other end of the rope pulled her back into the grass and nearly sent her sprawling. As the car slowly eased away, the unknown visitor turned and rolled down the window. And he smiled, baring white, even teeth that parted in laughter when Witch pushed Beth with her nose. A shock of recognition swept over her, even as her mind insisted it was impossible. But a scene from Charley's favorite television show flashed through her mind. Slick back the man's wavy hair and he could pass for the star's twin brother. But before she could convince herself she'd imagined the resemblance, the man looked away.

As the car rounded the corner out of sight, she forced her gaping mouth closed and tugged on the end of the rope. The cow followed with slow, grudging steps, stopping now and then for a bite of grass. Some fifteen minutes later, Beth and the cow rounded the corner and strode past the house. Seeing the blue car parked squarely in their path, the cow halted and refused to budge. Beth glared in irritation at the trio conversing animatedly beside the car.

"Charley!" she called softly. "Talk to her."

Glancing around, Charley surmised the situation

immediately and resumed his singsong chant as he strolled toward the cow.

"Watch this," Marlene cooed, while she stroked a necklace of chunky wooden beads. "He's simply amazing. He's even better with animals than my daughter."

Watching her mother flutter and preen herself, Beth sighed and shook her head. It was always the same. Her hard-nosed, practical mother put on a silly canary act around men as she flattered them and pretended a dependence and fragility that was so far removed from reality that it was laughable.

Turning deliberately away from them, Beth concentrated on Witch, and with Charley's help, coaxed her past the car.

"Beth, darling," Marlene coaxed. "Let Charley take care of the cow. I want you to meet Justin."

Beth paused and stole a glance at the man, then relaxed. She had imagined it. Granted, this Justin was attractive, but his hair was too dark. She'd bet, too, that those casual, baggy clothes hid more than a few sagging muscles. He was just another well-bred lawyer or accountant that Marlene, in her desperation, had brought to meet Beth. All considered, he was fairly ordinary, except for his unusually blue eyes.

She handed the rope over to Charley, but didn't comply any further than that. She smiled uncomfortably and nodded, murmuring welcoming platitudes, just like her grandmother had taught her when she was a little girl. When Justin would have taken her hand, she held up her dirty palms and murmured an apology, glad of the excuse. She wished he'd turn those laughing eyes on Witch, or even back on Marlene. Bristling, Beth lifted her chin and pasted on the false smile she used when dealing with most of Marlene's friends, then interrupted the gushing chatter.

"Go on up to the house," Beth told her mother. "I'll be there in a few minutes, after I've put the tools away. We can talk then."

"Can I help?" Justin offered.

Beth's eyes swept down the casually tailored suit to the polished leather shoes. "You're not dressed for the barn."

He shrugged. "It's only dirt."

"Not quite," Charley warned. "But if you want to do it, I'd appreciate the help. My hip's not feeling too good right now."

She studied the old man's face and noticed the signs of strain, the deepened wrinkles, and the pasty gray of his skin. "Go on, Charley. We'll manage," she said.

Turning to Justin, her false smile changed to one of anticipation. The man had laughed at her, was still laughing at her with those expressive eyes. Her turn would come, though, in just a few minutes when he stepped those impeccably shined shoes into a barnyard of manure.

She'd seen enough of his kind in the five years since her mother had married into money. For the first year, she'd lived with her mother and Alfred, her stepfather. On her eighteenth birthday, she'd moved back home to the farm to live with Grandma and Great Aunt Eva, Grandma's sister. After Grandma died, leaving the farm to Beth, it was impossible to think of living anywhere else. Since then, Beth had visited Marlene and Alfred periodically and endured the attentions of the young lawyers and doctors and businessmen they'd introduced her to. But she didn't fit into their world, and they certainly didn't fit into hers. Surreptitiously stealing a look at Justin's smooth hands curled around Witch's rope, she experienced a niggling guilt, but she suppressed it quickly. He'd offered to help. She'd warned him. If he ruined his expensive clothes, it wouldn't be her fault.

"Why don't you knock off for the day, too, Beth?" Charley suggested. "Let one of the boys do the milking."

She nodded silently, then turned toward the barn. The two high school students were planting sweet corn in one of the back fields. She knew they'd finish soon and would check in with her. Looking back, she saw Justin throw his jacket and tie into the car and roll up his shirtsleeves. Then he tugged lightly on the rope, urging Witch to follow. Beth eyed Witch warily, but the cow trundled placidly along behind Justin. Intrigued, Beth surveyed the man who had inspired such obedience, then flushed when he caught her stare.

"Your mother said this farm's been in the family for three generations. Does the line stop with you, or are there more Thompsons to carry on?" Justin asked.

Beth considered ignoring what she considered an intrusive question, then decided there was no harm in answering. "Just me. I inherited it when my grandmother died. I guess she figured I'd keep it going."

"No husband?"

"I'm sure my mother already filled you in on my marital state," she replied wryly.

"So you and Charley run the place."

"Something like that. He worked for my grandmother for years." She gestured toward Witch, who was hanging back.

He jerked the rope, pulling the cow away from a bed of newly planted flowers. Sunlight flashed off his Rolex watch with the motion, and a flash of black whipped past.

A few seconds later, Edgar landed on Beth's shoulder and shrieked a hoarse imitation of a peacock. She winced and looked over to find Justin staring wide-eyed at her, or at Edgar. She couldn't tell which since Edgar's beak was practically in her ear.

"This is Edgar," she explained. "He doesn't know he's a crow. Charley gave him to my grandmother when he was a tiny chick, and she raised him in a box on the porch."

Justin shook his head as if to clear the cobwebs. "That sound he just made. I've never heard a crow squawk like that."

Beth chuckled. "That's his peacock call. He also does chickens, geese, and people."

"He talks?"

"Not with words like a parrot would. But he imitates voices and sounds pretty well."

Justin scratched his head, and the watch flashed reflected light again. Edgar chortled, then coasted from Beth's shoulder to Justin's arm and pecked at the shiny watchband.

"What the hell!" Justin shouted as he jerked his arm about in an effort to dislodge the bird. Frightened by the commotion, Witch bellowed and jerked the rope out of Justin's hand. The cow made a mad dash for the barn, trampling through the herb bed on the way.

Both hands free now, Justin slapped at the bird. Realizing that the odds were against him, Edgar took refuge in a nearby tree and squawked his indignation. Beth surveyed the overturned sundial and trail of hoofprints with dismay while her anger built into a slow simmer.

"Damned crazy bird," Justin was muttering behind her.

She spun around. "Get that watch off before he goes after you again," she ordered. "The ring, too, just to be on the safe side."

Justin looked away from the angry red scratches on his arm and stared at her as if she'd lost her mind. "What?"

"Your watch. Crows like anything shiny. Didn't my mother warn you?"

He frowned, but she met his glare with one of her own. "She warned me about a lot of things before we got here," he said. "But she didn't mention an attack bird."

Beth closed the distance between them and lifted his arm. His hand on hers was warm, shockingly warm and firm beneath her touch. Ignoring the subtle sensations that crept through her nervous system, she surveyed the scratches. "You'd better get these cleaned right away. Go on up to the house and ask Aunt Eva for some disinfectant. She'll take care of you."

"What about the cow?"

"Witch?" Beth said stupidly, then realized she was still holding his arm. She dropped it hastily and backed away. "I think I'll do better on my own, thank you." Then she turned and stalked toward the barn door where the cow was standing. She stole a glance over her shoulder, then turned back quickly when she saw he was still watching her, his face shadowed in the early-evening sunlight.

She didn't look again until Witch was safely through the barn gate. He was gone, then, and some of the tension immediately left her shoulders. It should only have taken a few minutes to settle Witch down for the evening and feed old Brownie and the other horses. But she found herself stalling.

She wasn't up to dealing with Marlene, let alone with Justin's recriminations. He was probably ready to sue her by now for not controlling her pets. She wished she could slip in quietly and go straight to bed, but she doubted her mother would let her get away with that, even if Charley and Aunt Eva would.

So instead, she headed back toward the house and put on a sociable face. Fortunately, Marlene was alone on the front porch of the rambling Victorian farmhouse. It had seen better days, and was sorely in need of paint. But it was home.

"Where's your friend?" Beth asked as she climbed the steps.

"Inside with Aunt Eva. I forgot to warn him about Edgar, I'm sorry to say," Marlene said, enfolding her daughter in a warm hug. Beth relaxed, her irritation temporarily forgotten. Her arms tightened around her mother for an instant before releasing her and taking a seat on the porch swing.

"Next time you decide to bring a guest, call first and I'll lock the blasted bird up," she suggested.

Her mother joined her on the swing, handing over one of the glasses of tea she held.

"Thanks, Mother. How bad are the scratches?" Beth asked, then raised the glass to her lips.

"Edgar didn't do too much damage, but that doesn't change the fact that your bird attacked your date. I know you're going to have a heck of a time smoothing that over."

Beth swallowed hard, narrowly avoiding a choking fit. "My date? Mother, what are you talking about?"

"Justin. He's your date for the weekend." She

flashed a Cheshire grin, then frowned. "You're not upset, are you? No, don't answer that. You called me 'Mother,' and you only slip up and call me that when you're upset."

Beth ignored that. "He didn't ask me for a date. And if he had, I'd have turned him down."

"You'd turn down Justin Kyle? Darlin', you must be running a fever."

A chill raced down Beth's spine. "Kyle? Justin Kyle?"

"Well, that's not his real name, dear, but that's what he goes by. That's what they put in the credits."

"He's not—" The words stuck in her throat. Her first impression had been right.

"Of course he is. I know Charley watches 'Vice Cops.' Aunt Eva, too. Don't you ever watch it with them? Anyway, I bought him for you. He's yours for the whole weekend." Marlene's brows pinched together for an instant. "Well, not yours exactly, but for all intents and purposes—"

"You *what?*" Beth interrupted. "What do you mean you bought him? You don't buy people."

"I did," Marlene insisted. "I paid ten thousand dollars for him at a charity auction today. And I think he was a bargain—or at least he could be if you'd use the brains God gave you."

Beth's head dropped into her hands and she groaned. "Was this one of those fancy auctions where men strut around on stage while a bunch of rich women drink martinis and bid on them?"

"Mimosas, dear. Martinis taste nasty. Anyway, it's all for charity. The money goes to a shelter for the homeless. And it was such a coup for the club to get Justin Kyle. We had plenty of local men—newscasters, football players, even a city councilman. But someone as well known as Justin was bound to bring a high price. I'll have to admit, I had a devil of a time getting him for you. The bidding was hectic."

Beth just shook her head and stared at the woman. Marlene had always been flamboyant in her own way, even when they'd been dirt poor. Since she'd married Alfred, she'd been able to buy the things she'd always dreamed about. Alfred didn't seem to mind paying her bills, not even flinching when she splurged on new wardrobes for herself and Beth. In fact, he seemed to enjoy indulging her. But this was different.

"Mother, what is Alfred going to say?"

Marlene frowned, then wiped the expression away with a wave of her hand. "Oh, he won't mind. He was just saying the other day how important that shelter is to the community. Now, you're going to have to do something about those clothes. And that strange smell, what is it?"

"What smell?" Beth sniffed. "Oh. Sage, basil, mint, I guess. I was working in the herb bed this afternoon. I'll shower before dinner."

"Good, and put on that lovely turquoise dress I gave you for your birthday. You'll need to look nice for Justin tonight. There might be reporters around at the Duck Club."

"I'm not going out with him."

"Well, you have to, dear," Marlene declared indignantly. "I paid a lot of money for him."

"I don't care how much you paid for him. I don't want him. Take him back." Beth's arms crossed defiantly and she glared at her mother.

"I can't."

"Take him back," Beth repeated firmly.

"Why? He's perfect."

Beth glared. "If he's so perfect, *you* keep him. *You* bought him, for Pete's sake."

Marlene frowned. "I might be tempted, but he's too young for me. Besides, I'm leaving tonight for Paris. Alfred's about to finish his business there, and he's promised to take some time off. Don't you think it would be lovely to summer in Europe?"

Not to be distracted, Beth pointed to the car. "Good idea. Pack Justin Kyle up and take him along. Take him to the moon for all I care. Just get him out of here."

She turned on her heel and marched across the porch and into the house, slamming the screen door. Her mother was fast behind her.

"Try to be reasonable, Beth."

"Me? Mother, when and if I need a man, I'll find one the old-fashioned way. I'll go to the church picnic. Now just take him back to town and send him back to California or wherever he came from."

"She can't." Justin's voice startled them both. While Marlene flushed with embarrassment, Beth simply glared.

"Why not?" she asked.

"If we don't go on this date, then the shelter will have to refund the money. Ten thousand dollars will buy a lot of beds and a lot of hamburger." He didn't know how true this was, but it sounded convincing.

"You're joking! I'm letting you off the hook and you're not cooperating."

He shook his head and stifled a childish urge to cross his fingers against the lie he was considering. This spicy redhead had caught his eye the minute she'd angrily marched down that hill after the cow. Her green eyes had flashed fire and she'd moved with an athletic grace that made him think of the smoothly muscled legs he knew hid beneath those tight, tattered jeans. He'd noticed, too, as she'd stalked away from him later that her rear end had an enticing twitch when she was angry. She promised to be an interesting diversion in a very boring publicity tour—if she or one of her pets didn't maim him first.

First, though, she had to cooperate. **Gen**tle persuasion and seductive smiles wouldn't work with her. He suspected, though, that her tough exterior hid a soft heart. Why else would she live here with this menagerie of offbeat creatures when her mother obviously had the means to provide better accommodations.

"We both have to go through with this," he said finally. "It's in the contract. If I don't show up with you for the publicity shots, the deal's off. A lot of poor people lose their dinner, and I lose my good reputation."

Beth's hands rested on her hips. "So this is a publicity stunt?"

Justin shrugged. "It wasn't my idea. My contract with the network calls for a number of personal appearances to be arranged by their staff. They set this up." That much, at least, was true.

Beth's expression turned speculative. "So what's the worst that could happen if we don't show? And don't give me that baloney about the shelter returning the money to Marlene. Marlene can donate the money outright without all this auction nonsense."

Justin took a deep breath and expelled it, wincing inwardly at Beth's persistent rejection. For several years now, he'd only needed to smile and let the dimples and his star status do the rest. But Beth Ann Thompson seemed immune to his much-touted charm, and he was intrigued. Very intrigued. Somehow he had to convince her to have dinner with him that night. His racing pulse and cramped breath warned him that there was more to this than the challenge, but he refused to listen to that inner voice.

"Part of the contract stipulates that, in return for the publicity, the network will match the winning bid," Justin said.

Marlene gasped. "I didn't realize that. Beth, darling, I'd be happy to just donate the ten thousand. But twenty? I can only ask so much of Alfred."

"You bought him. You go out with him."

Marlene paled. "I couldn't, Beth Ann. Think what would happen if Alfred picked up the morning paper and saw a picture of me and Justin. Darling, you know how jealous he gets."

"You should have thought of that before the auction."

"I did. I registered under your name."

"You *what*? How could you?" Beth sank into a faded armchair and stared blankly ahead of her. "Wait a minute. You couldn't pull that off. Too many people know you."

"Well, of course. And I signed my own name to the check, too. But I registered in your name, and those are the papers the publicity people took."

Beth closed her eyes and groaned. She felt trapped, and they all knew it. Trapped by her mother's manipulations, and, face it, by her own conscience. She could just imagine what a difference another ten thousand dollars would make to the shelter. Besides, it was only one evening.

"All right, I give up," she said. "When and where should I meet you?"

"Beth Ann Thompson!" The simpering canary act

slipped, and Beth detected the underlying steel will of the real Marlene. "I will drive you there. You're not getting the chance to welch on this deal."

"I wouldn't!" Beth insisted, but her mother's knowing expression said she believed otherwise.

"All right. You can follow me. Or better yet," Beth said, turning to Justin, "can you drive a stick shift?"

Thrown off balance by the question, he knit his brows in puzzlement. "Well, it's been a while. Why?"

"I have work to do tomorrow. If you drive my pickup, I can nap on the way to the city. Also, I'll have no problem getting back here to the farm tonight."

"Take my car," Marlene offered, wrinkling her nose. "It's clean, and it doesn't smell like fertilizer."

"I thought you were going to Paris," Beth said.

"I am, but my flight isn't until midnight. You'll be back in plenty of time, won't you? And if you're not, Charley can drive me to the airport. Besides, I'm looking forward to a nice long chat with Aunt Eva."

Beth eyed her mother suspiciously, knowing that Marlene and Aunt Eva fought constantly. Even now, she suspected Aunt Eva was hiding in the kitchen to avoid a confrontation. It was obvious what her mother was up to. Marlene had maneuvered her into a date with America's heartthrob, and now she was smoothing the path for romance. Beth would have laughed, the situation was so ridiculous. But she knew that despite Marlene's extravagant manipulations, the woman really meant well. Marlene had never been meant to live alone, and couldn't understand how her daughter could be happy without a man to take care of her.

Beth had quit explaining years ago. True, she'd like to have a family someday. But there weren't many men who could accept her as she was instead of trying to mold her into their idea of what a wife should be. Those who could were usually forty years too old or calf-eyed adolescents.

Her gaze slipped away from Marlene to Justin, who was tapping his thumbs together above laced fingers. He must have felt her attention on him, because he looked up suddenly, catching her unawares. Then his lips curved into a smile. And in his eyes there was sympathy and a shared understanding for aging parents who felt the ticking of the biological clock more than their offspring.

She grinned wryly and gave a slow nod. One evening wouldn't hurt. Besides, it would be something to tell her grandchildren, if she ever got around to having any.

"All right," she finally agreed. "I'll get my purse and we can leave."

Marlene blocked the doorway. "Why don't you take a shower first?"

"Don't worry. I won't show up at the Peppercorn Duck Club with dirt on my face and manure on my boots. We'll have to stop by your place to change. All my good clothes are there."

"Why?"

"I only need them there." She couldn't resist a wink. "Have fun while I'm gone. I'll be back before you know it."

Marlene shook her head. "You're not getting in my car until you've had a shower. It's brand-new, and I won't have it smelling like that cow."

Beth sniffed. "I smell that bad?"

She could have sworn the corners of Justin's mouth twitched, but he fixed a bland expression on his face. "Come closer and I'll check."

"Never mind, I'll take a shower."

TWO

By the time Beth had showered and slipped on a clean T-shirt and jeans, her mood had mellowed somewhat. It wouldn't hurt to spend a couple of hours with him, she reasoned. They'd eat dinner, pose for a few photos, then go their separate ways. It was a small sacrifice to make for such a good cause.

"You've almost convinced yourself. But it's still not too late to back out," she muttered, then spun around when a hoarse voice mimicked her words.

"Edgar, who let you in?" The bird cocked his head, then swooped over to the bed and pecked a metal ring on her purse strap. "Go away. You've caused enough trouble already." Beth stepped over to the open window and examined the torn screen. It was past repair. A push, then a quick tug sent it, frame and all, tumbling down to the bushes. She'd drag it out to the barn before she left, then fix it tomorrow.

Edgar was chattering to himself in the mirror when she turned around. She shooed the crow through the torn screen before he could do any further damage. Then she closed and locked the window behind him.

An instant before she turned away, she noticed the movement by her mother's car.

Justin and Marlene stepped into view. Curious, Beth peered through the rippled glass of the old window, watching them shake hands. Then they talked for a moment, or rather Marlene talked, gesturing extravagantly. Justin just nodded and reached for the car door.

Beth's spirits lifted. *He'd changed his mind. He was leaving.* Her sense of relief died when Marlene slid into the driver's seat and waved to Justin. He backed away as Marlene slammed the door shut and revved the engine. He wasn't leaving, at least not with Marlene. At that moment, Beth realized that Marlene had no intention of giving her daughter the slightest chance to back out of this so-called date.

Beth's fingers fumbled on the lock, then jerked the window open. "Marlene, don't you dare leave," she bellowed. Two other faces appeared around the corner of the house. Charley and Aunt Eva stared up at the second-floor window, both grinning. But she had no time for them as she watched the car turn around and head down the drive.

"Marlene," she shouted again. "Mother!"

Charley's jaw dropped.

"You're lucky Marlene couldn't hear that," Aunt Eva shouted back. "She'd wash your mouth out."

Beth slammed the window closed. She grabbed her purse and headed down the stairs. Justin was just coming in the front door.

"Ready?" he asked.

"Why did she leave?"

"She remembered an errand."

Beth clenched her teeth. It wouldn't do any good just

now to point out that Marlene had probably planned this the moment she first bid on Justin at that auction.

"Having second thoughts?"

Beth's frown deepened as she lifted her chin. "What do you think?"

He leaned back against the door and eyed her soberly. "You really don't have to do this if it makes you that uncomfortable. It was your mother's idea, not yours."

"And she's run off to Paris leaving me to clean up the mess she's made," Beth answered.

"The decision is yours."

"What about your contract?"

He shrugged. "I have a good agent. He could smooth things over."

"He'll blame me."

"So? What can he do to you?"

Beth sagged down onto the bottom step and lowered her head into her hands. "There's still the matter of the studio's share of the donation. No, I'd feel too guilty if I didn't go with you."

"You're denting my ego," Justin replied.

"Sorry. It's nothing personal, but it was a bad day before Marlene showed up. This—this scheme of hers is the worst yet."

"Does this kind of thing happen to you often?" he asked.

"No, thank goodness. Usually she blackmails me into visiting her in the city, and just happens to invite somebody who's single and either rich or trying to get that way. But I guess she's getting desperate."

Justin made a choking sound, and Beth's eyes lifted to his face. He was laughing again, not aloud, but his eyes danced with barely suppressed merriment. Maybe later, years later, she'd laugh, too, at the way Marlene had outsmarted her this time. Right now, the humor of the situation eluded her.

The step creaked as he sat next to her. "I have to admit I've never had a day like this before," he said.

The wry amusement in his tone unexpectedly struck a responsive chord as her eyes met his. "You can't be enjoying this, either," she said. "I know this is just part of your job, but you're taking all of this craziness rather well. I thought actors were temperamental."

His grin widened. "I'm afraid that if I'm not nice, you'll sic that bird on me again. Then we'll spend the evening in the emergency room instead of a restaurant, and a lot of hungry people will get hungrier, myself included."

"About my mother . . . ." she began, but Justin's two fingers on her lips effectively halted her words. Light as a caress and heated against her flesh, they touched and held until she was speechless.

"Don't worry about it," he insisted. "She's not any nuttier than some of the people I work with." He leaned a bit closer and traced the line of her cheek until he reached and lifted her chin. His voice dropped to a husky persuasion. "So, will you come?"

The early-evening sunlight glinted through the window behind him, backlighting his hair with a blond halo. With his face shadowed in the dramatic lighting, he was the man she'd first recognized, the strikingly attractive star who chased bad guys across the TV screen on Tuesday nights. She remembered then that Justin was an actor, skilled at feigning sincerity. *How many times had he practiced those words, that dulcet tone, on screen and off? Was he acting now?*

She couldn't tell, but the very idea brought her

sharply down to earth. She drew a deep, almost angry breath before speaking. "I don't like being used, and I don't like being manipulated. If it weren't for those homeless people, I'd tell you and Marlene both to jump into the lake."

Justin leaned back, puzzlement written across his handsome features. "I guess that's a yes."

Beth glared, then leaped to her feet and headed for the kitchen. "Aunt Eva?"

"I hope you left enough hot water to wash dishes," the old woman answered. "You certainly dragged your feet getting down here. It's not smart to keep a good-looking man waiting." Two pork chops dangled from the older woman's fingertips, then dropped with a poof into a plate of flour.

Dinner for two, featuring all of Charley's favorites, I'll bet. "Is that chocolate cake I smell?" Beth peered through the oven door and reached for the handle, but Aunt Eva slapped her fingers away, leaving a dusting of flour behind.

"I'll save you a piece. Now off with you before that nice young man gets tired of waiting and leaves without you."

Stifling a grin, Beth brushed away the flour. "I'll be back around ten. Tell Charley we'll start clearing the north greenhouse tomorrow."

"Tell him yourself. He's out getting the truck ready. He figured you'd want to leave the fertilizer and the old pump here." Eva held out a grease-spotted slip of paper. "On your way home in the morning, could you pick up a few things?"

Beth tucked the paper into her pocket and reached for the bucket of milk sitting by the refrigerator. "I'll just strain the milk and put it away for you. By the way, did you take care of that insurance problem and send them copies of the canceled checks? That should convince them you paid the premium."

"Off with you now," Aunt Eva said, snapping a dish towel at Beth. "Don't I always do what needs doing? Now go, before that man slips away."

Beth snorted, but refused to be baited. She dropped a light kiss on Aunt Eva's papery cheek. "Mmm. New perfume?"

"Soap," the older woman retorted tartly. "Might try it yourself a bit more often instead of grubbing around in the dirt like a farmhand."

Beth grinned. "I *am* a farmhand," she replied, ignoring Aunt Eva's muffled hummph as she stepped into the pantry and rustled around. Another grunt was her only answer to Beth's farewell call.

Justin was no longer at the stairs. Nor was he on the front porch. Beth finally found him behind the barn helping Charley unload the heavy irrigation pump.

"Where are the boys?" she asked.

"Gone home for supper," Charley growled, then set his end down with a thump and rubbed his lower back. "Damn thing gets heavier every year."

A streak of grease marred Justin's shirtfront, and there was a matching smudge on one trouser leg. "Where do you want it?"

"Right there's fine. The boys can put it into the shed in the morning," she said. "Thanks for your help."

"What if it rains?"

"Won't hurt it," Charley interjected. "You'd best be findin' a rag and be on your way or that restaurant'll be locked up afore you get there."

Justin stopped at the front of the truck and touched

the piece of equipment attached there. "What about the winch?"

Beth raised her brows. At least the man wasn't a total idiot about machinery, not if he recognized a winch. "It can stay there. It's too much trouble to take off and put back on," she said.

She led him into the barn and showed him where to wash up, then returned to the truck to clear out the cab. She had just finished storing the assorted hand tools and bags of seeds when Justin joined her.

"Ready?" he asked.

"As I'll ever be." She climbed in behind the wheel.

"I thought you wanted to sleep."

"No, I was stalling until I could come up with a good excuse. Unfortunately, I struck out." She slammed the door shut and jammed down the clutch before turning the key. The ignition chugged to life, but Justin made no move to get in. His lips moved, but she couldn't hear him over the noise of the truck.

Sighing, she cut the engine. "What did you say?"

Justin leaned against the door, practically through the open window. "How about a truce?"

"I wasn't aware that I was at war with you. With Marlene, maybe. But you're just a bystander."

"I'm getting shot in the crossfire," he said, sincerity written across his face.

Beth felt her insides curl tighter, then slowly relax as the faint lines about his eyes creased into a warm smile. *He must have practiced that expression for hours.* Despite the mental reminder, she felt herself soften toward him.

"Get in," she said. "I'll behave."

His devilish grin indicated he'd rather she didn't. He'd probably perfected that expression in front of the mirror as well, she thought. Chances are, he used it quite often.

She restarted the engine and headed toward the highway as soon as Justin's door closed. The noise from the truck made conversation virtually impossible, so it wasn't until they reached the city limits that she spoke.

"Which hotel?" she shouted.

"The Hyatt. That's where we're eating, too."

"I'll drop you off, then meet you after I've changed."

"Promise? You won't just turn around and go home?"

"Promise." When she smiled at him, she caught the flickering reflection of the dying light in his eyes, and something else she didn't dare try to identify. Nevertheless, the pickup cab felt suddenly warm, despite the open windows.

She left him at the front entrance after agreeing to meet him at that same spot at eight o'clock, then maneuvered the noisy pickup through the crowded streets to the Country Club Plaza. She wasn't surprised that both the doorman and the garage attendant at Marlene's building were expecting her. The housekeeper was out, but either she or Marlene had laid out the turquoise jacquard dress. Drop-dead gorgeous, Marlene had said when Beth tried it on the first time. It also exposed too much bare flesh, if she remembered correctly. She riffled through the closet until she found her favorite green silk, then quickly tossed off her jeans and T-shirt. Rummaging through the lingerie drawer, she finally located a lace-edged slip, but all the panty hose seemed to have disappeared.

Feeling a bit decadent, she slipped on a pink garter and the barely-there chemise and panties someone had left out with the turquoise dress. It took only a few moments to apply makeup, comb her mass of curls, and locate the spike-heeled sandals. After putting on the full-skirted green dress, she spent a few minutes walking around the penthouse, practicing in the heels like a teenager until she grew accustomed to the feel of them.

She was almost to the elevator when she decided to borrow one of Alfred's cars. Suddenly she didn't want to arrive at the Hyatt like a country hick in an exhaust-belching pickup. She let herself back into the penthouse, found the keys to the Jaguar, then headed for the garage.

She reached the Hyatt ten minutes late and nudged the Jaguar into a spot between the airport shuttle van and the curb. As she handed her keys to the parking attendant, she spotted Justin at the revolving door with a harried-looking brunette in tow. He grimaced as a camera flashed in his face, blinked hard, and glanced around, scanning the parking lot and the street beyond. She realized he must be looking for the pickup truck. Then she pursed her lips and emitted a sharp whistle to draw his attention.

A dozen startled pairs of eyes glanced her way, and she grinned impishly from behind the Jaguar. The airport van pulled away and she immediately felt the breeze the van had blocked. As she rounded the rear of the Jaguar, a sudden gust caught the green silk, which fluttered around her legs, then whipped over her face and around her hair before she could grab it. While she clutched at the skirt of her dress, she felt the wind on her legs, high above where her slip should have covered.

It was only a matter of seconds before she had the dress under control, but her dignity was not so easily regained. She slumped against the car for an instant, muttering a series of expletives, then forced her eyes open.

"Nice legs," the parking attendant commented, then slid into the Jaguar and revved the engine. Holding the skirt firmly, Beth edged away from the car and crossed the pavement. The dozen pairs of eyes that had stared were now turned discreetly away, though everyone seemed to be struggling not to laugh. One older gentleman strove vainly for a nonchalant whistle that ended in a teary chuckle.

Suddenly the humor of the situation overrode her embarrassment, and a smile crept across her face. She straightened her spine and made her way to where Justin and the brunette stood. "Sorry I'm late," she said.

"That's quite an entrance," Justin said, eyes twinkling.

Beth felt her blush deepen and was surprised that was even possible. "Bad dress choice," she murmured.

"No, that color is perfect for you. The rest was just the wind—careless of you maybe, but it happens," the other woman said.

"It livens things up a bit," Justin added, then began the introductions. "Mel, meet Beth. Beth, this is my—"

Before he could finish, a flash went off in their faces.

"Will you people just save it until the press conference?" the brunette snapped and led the photographer away, with the help of a hotel security guard.

"Press conference?" Beth drew a deep breath. "You said publicity photos. Nobody told me they'd be asking questions."

"There'll be a couple of reporters, but it's not really a press conference," Justin assured her. "Mel just said that to get the creep away from you."

"That's right. I didn't mean to upset you," the brunette said as she rejoined them and touched Justin's arm. He smiled and covered her hand with his free one for an instant.

So that's how things lie. Or are all Californians so touchy-feely.

The brunette finally sent a harried glance her way. "I'm Melanie Adams, Justin's publicist," she said, handing Beth a sheaf of papers.

"The top one is a brief bio on you—everything we could put together on such short notice. Then there's the press release, and sample questions and answers. Now, if you'll follow me, we can get started. I'd hoped to have more time to brief you on what to expect, but since you were late you'll just have to wing it. If you get nervous, just read directly from the press release." Her lips twisted into what was probably meant to be a smile as she led the way to the elevator and punched a button.

As they sped upward, Beth studied the papers and wished her stomach would settle. For a single, panicked instant, the words swam on the page, then settled into a jumbled mismatch of letters that made no sense. In her mind, she was back in grade school, stumbling over her reading assignment and enduring the whispered taunts of her classmates, who always were so much smarter, who seemed to absorb the words effortlessly.

No. She was past that now. Two years in an expensive private school had changed all that. Highly paid professionals had done what the overworked remedial-room teacher at her old school hadn't had enough time or motivation to do. She stared at the page again and the letters settled into place. She flipped to the page of cleverly worded questions and answers. They all made perfect sense, even if they were vague. Well, if politicians could do it, so could she. Maybe. If she didn't panic.

It was obvious that Melanie intended for Beth to use the papers as crib sheets, in case her mind blanked under pressure. But the bio didn't include one simple fact—dyslexia. Beth had overcome the dyslexia itself, but not the fears that years of childhood difficulties had imbedded in her mind. She read slowly, still stumbling sometimes over the words. But she couldn't read aloud in front of a group of reporters if her life depended upon it.

Think about something else, she told herself. She looked away and found herself witness to a silent conversation. When Melanie shook her head in answer to Justin's unspoken question, his features stiffened, deepening the lines on his brow. Feeling uncomfortably like an eavesdropper, Beth looked away.

The elevator stopped at the eighth floor and Melanie whisked through the doors as soon as they opened. Beth hesitated, but Justin's hand on her lower spine was enough to jar her into movement. His touch was light, but she was more conscious of it than the floor beneath her feet.

Melanie paused just outside a door and waited for the others to catch up. Through the half-open door, Beth could see a stretch of thick carpeting leading to an overstuffed sofa. "The studio photographer's already set up," she said. "There's a couple of reporters, one from the Kansas City Star and another from a radio station—they'll have a few questions for you while the photographer works. Then there's Bob Greeno." Her voice dripped with revulsion.

"Who's that?" Beth asked, afraid of the answer.

"The creep who was out front with the camera,"

Justin supplied. "He's a freelancer, mostly for the sleaze press."

"Tabloids," Melanie explained. "They pay big money for celebrity photos."

"Why was he invited?"

Melanie frowned. "He wasn't. But it's better to work with him than make him angry. He could really damage Justin's career if he decided to get nasty. A word of advice—don't mention the crow attack."

Did the woman think she was stupid? "That would certainly get their attention," Beth quipped and added a silly grin for effect, figuring she might as well play the part Melanie expected.

Justin reached around the two women for the door handle. "Let's get this over with. I'm hungry," he said. Melanie rolled her eyes and led the way into the room.

The photo session wasn't as bad as Beth had anticipated. A makeup artist touched up her face, adding several layers more makeup than Beth liked, then glued on false fingernails. The hair stylist took one look at the mop of red curls and lifted her scissors. "If I just trimmed a bit off the top," she suggested. Beth's glare stopped her before she could snip a single strand, and at Melanie's nod, the stylist disappeared into the corridor.

"Somebody told them I'm a farmer, I'll bet," Beth said after the woman had left. Her eyes sparked with indignation. "Which places me slightly above the garbage man in fashion sense."

Justin shrugged. "That's not your problem."

"Usually not," she agreed, then fluttered the blood-red nails between them. "I hope the glue is temporary. Otherwise I'll shred more seedlings than I'll plant tomorrow."

"Tomorrow's Saturday," Melanie reminded her.

Beth smiled. "That's when we get the most done. It's the only time this month that the high school kids I hired can work a full day."

Melanie nodded distractedly, then answered the knock at the door. Murmuring a brief apology to the group in general, she disappeared into the hallway. Beth watched for her return, but the woman stayed away. Perhaps she didn't want to watch him pander to another woman, no matter how insincere his effort was. That would explain her absence.

After nearly an hour of posing for the camera, turning this way and that, standing, sitting, even jumping, the photographer turned off the lights and pronounced himself satisfied with the shots. "I'll get a few more candid shots at the restaurant and afterward."

While he packed up his equipment, Justin parried the reporters' questions, smoothing the way for Beth. Ignoring the crib sheets lying on a table a few feet away, she quelled her nervousness and marshaled her thoughts. She answered the questions put directly to her with little trouble, explaining her mother's devotion to charitable causes and the reason she couldn't be there herself.

"And you're a farmer?" a reporter asked in a bored tone.

Beth nodded and explained briefly what Thompson Farm produced. Finding nothing particularly interesting about Beth, the reporters' questions strayed away from her and the auction to Justin's plans for the hiatus in "Vice Cops" taping.

"I'll be working on an adventure film in Mexico during part of the hiatus," he explained. "And I'm reviewing several scripts my agent sent, but nothing else is definite.''

"Justin . . ." Bob Greeno, the rude photographer began. "Rumor has it that you won't be with 'Vice Cops' next season."

Justin's easy grin reflected amusement, but Beth noticed that the lines around his eyes didn't crinkle like they had when he'd smiled at her—or at Melanie.

"You know how rumors are, Bob," Justin said. "You create enough of them."

Greeno leered, oblivious to the tittering laughter around him. "That doesn't answer my question. Are the producers canning you?"

"No. And I have no plans to leave the show," Justin answered, and stifled the sudden childish desire to cross his fingers against the lie. He had plans, nothing definite, but he was tired of the macho typecast parts he'd played, both in the TV series and in the movies he'd been offered. He'd told his agent to keep an eye open for something a bit more serious, something challenging. One script looked promising, but his agent thought the film didn't have enough backing, that it probably wouldn't be made.

Suddenly tired of all the show and pretense, Justin stood up and held out his hand to Beth. "If there are no more questions . . ." he added in a firm, but pleasant tone, "we have dinner reservations. I haven't eaten since the flight this morning and, frankly, I'm famished."

She took his hand, smiled at the reporters, endured a few more photo flashes, then followed him into the corridor. Closing the door behind him, Justin heaved an exaggerated sigh of relief.

"My sentiments exactly," Beth agreed. "By the

way, where's Melanie? I would have thought she'd be there to help handle the reporters."

"You did fine," Justin insisted, though privately he, too, wondered what had kept Mel away. It wasn't like her.

The elevator was empty as they stepped inside. Leaning against the opposite wall, he surveyed Beth's carefully sculptured hair and makeup and decided he liked the way she'd looked this afternoon better. She'd appeared open and honest then, straightforward to the point of bluntness. She'd been easy to read. This sophisticated redhead across from him hid secrets beneath her half-closed lids. She'd been so cool, so composed up there in the suite. He fought a half-baked notion to upset that composure and see what happened. Temptation won.

"I seduced a gorgeous blonde in an elevator in *Day of Revenge*," he said.

"I know. Lucky for you I'm not a blonde."

"You saw the movie?"

She shook her head. "Not yet."

"It's out on videocassette now."

Beth bit her lip and glanced at the ceiling. "Aunt Eva told me about it. She said it was disgusting, obscene, and a few other things that aren't so nice."

Justin winced. "No wonder she hid in the kitchen this afternoon. I'm surprised she didn't paint a red 'A' on my chest with the Merthiolate."

"She was avoiding Marlene. And I wouldn't worry about what Aunt Eva says."

"Why not? She didn't enjoy the movie because it offended her. Although between you and me, I'm not that surprised. There wasn't much plot to it."

Beth smirked. "That's what she said. But she

watched it three times with Charley. Though I wonder whether the attraction was you or Charley.''

Justin raised his brows. ''It's Aunt Eva, but not Uncle Charley?''

''Not yet,'' Beth said with a straight face. ''But they've been courting as long as I can remember.'' Her serious expression slipped when Justin laughed outright.

When the doors opened, he pulled her into the corridor and led her to the entrance to the Peppercorn Duck Club.

They were quickly seated, and though a few heads turned their way, no one stared or even paid them any particular attention. Relieved not to be the spectacle she'd expected, Beth began to relax.

''This is one of my favorite restaurants,'' she commented as she looked over the menu, then quickly set it aside, her decision already made.

Glancing over the top of the menu, Justin had to admit that the Beth Thompson across from him fit the softly lit, elegant surroundings as if she was born to luxury. He was almost taken in until he noticed the muted tapping of the false nails, against the tabletop this time. ''But you'd rather be on the porch at home,'' he replied in a stage whisper.

The tapping stopped. ''It shows?''

''Not much.''

''It's not the company,'' she explained. ''And the food here is terrific. I guess I'm just not the social type.''

''What type are you?''

Her eyes locked with his. ''Isn't that obvious? I'm a country mouse in city clothing. When I leave the city, I leave all this behind me,'' she said, indicating her surroundings with a wave of her hand.

"A chameleon." It wasn't a question. He'd seen her blend into two vastly different settings. But he wondered which was the real Beth. The arrival of the waiter stalled any further questioning, and when they were alone again, she shifted the subject.

"Where are you from?"

"A tiny town in Illinois," he answered. "And I have the requisite parents, two brothers, and one sister. Just an average family." His tone didn't invite further questions, but that didn't faze Beth.

"So what do you do to amuse yourself when you aren't playing super cop?" Beth asked.

He shrugged. "Lots of things. Handball. Swimming."

"In a pool or in the ocean."

"Mostly in a pool. There's a place I get away to whenever I can, but the water isn't good for swimming there."

"Too polluted?"

"Too cold," he answered, then wondered why he'd said so much. He didn't want anyone to know about that place. He'd worked too hard to keep it hidden, and he didn't want to lose the one place he could escape to. But there was something about this woman that invited confidences, and he was afraid what those sparkling green eyes would coax out of him. So he subtly shifted the conversation to his work.

As he entertained her with amusing anecdotes about various filming mishaps, he absorbed the flickering emotions that crossed her face. Once, as they chose dessert from the chocolate cart, his eyes caught hers and held, and she unaccountably flushed. Then her eyes focused somewhere beyond his left shoulder, and sparks of green fire flashed, reminding him of the earthy, flustered woman he'd met that afternoon.

Turning to see what had disturbed her, Justin noticed the commotion at the entrance. A security guard had pinned Bob Greeno against the wall and was stripping a roll of film from his camera. Melanie hovered nearby, looking worried. She spoke to one of the waiters, smiled briefly, then crossed to their table.

"Justin, I need to speak to you for a moment. I wouldn't have interrupted your dinner, but it's important," she said. Her pale face against her near-black hair lent an exotic fragility that Beth hadn't noticed before.

"Excuse me," Justin said, then left Beth alone at the table.

They talked in the corridor out of earshot, but not out of sight, while Beth concentrated on the chocolate mousse on her plate. She risked a covert glance at the entryway just as Justin looked her way. He caught her eye and smiled. Heat coursed through her veins. *Idiot! Keep it in perspective! He can't help that smile any more than he can help breathing*.

Then he pointed to his lip. Puzzled, Beth stared, then shrugged. He touched his lip again, then pointed directly at her. She glanced around, but no one else seemed to be paying any attention to the odd exchange. When she touched her chin, he nodded, then pointed upward.

Good grief! She had food on her face.

She touched her lip with her tongue and tasted chocolate. Lots of it. She closed her eyes in embarrassment and reached for the napkin. As she opened them again, he was still staring and nodding absently at whatever Melanie had said. Beth unconsciously licked her lip again, then realized what she was doing as his smile faded and unmistakable desire smouldered in his eyes.

Then Melanie touched his arm and spoke. His lips mouthed "I'm sorry," but to Melanie, not Beth. A grim expression replaced the desire as his arms closed around Melanie. He kissed her hair, then released her and watched her leave.

The mousse lost its appeal. The exchange she just witnessed fueled her earlier uneasiness, and she felt like a third wheel. *How's that for perspective?* reminded the little voice in her head. Drawing circles in the half-eaten mousse, Beth pondered her situation. Basically, she was on a date that wasn't really a date, with a TV star who hid behind his public persona. He hadn't revealed a single personal detail. She didn't know how Melanie figured into the picture, either, but it was obvious that she was more than his publicist. Those two were tied together somehow—not married or he'd never have been in a bachelor auction—but connected nonetheless. And she wondered why the idea disturbed her so much.

Justin seemed subdued when he returned. "I'm sorry," he said as he sat down. "Something's come up and I'm going to have to leave tonight. I know this date was supposed to last through the weekend, but you'll be relieved to know I can't finish this out." He stabbed his fork halfheartedly at his chocolate cheesecake.

Beth swallowed, then reached for the water glass to wash away the tightness in her throat. "I have to work tomorrow anyway, remember?" she replied, her voice hoarser than she liked. "There won't be any problem with the studio's donation, will there?"

The fork stopped. "What donation?"

THREE

Beth's incredulous expression warned him that he'd made a major slip, one that would be harder to recover from than a missed cue on Broadway.

"You are worried," she continued, her green eyes darkening with concern. "Whatever is wrong must be bad if you've forgotten why we're stuck with each other for the evening. The studio's donation to the shelter for the homeless. Remember? The money they wouldn't get if I didn't show up here tonight."

Justin rubbed his forehead, staring at the melting puff of mousse next to the cheesecake. "Right. Sorry," he murmured, then reached for the spoon. He stifled the twinge of guilt he felt about lying to Beth, for continuing to deceive her. There was no matching clause in the contract, but the money didn't matter. He'd make the donation himself—he donated several times that amount every year to similar causes.

"Are you all right?" Beth's calloused fingertips brushed the back of his hand.

He drew a ragged breath and nodded.

"You're sure? You look a bit flushed."

"I'm fine," he insisted, his voice sharper than he'd intended. Beth jerked her hand away, her own color high.

He realized then which Beth was real—the warm, feisty farm woman from this afternoon. The sophisticated veneer barely disguised that side of her, and if he'd been paying attention, he'd have known it all along. At that moment, he felt shallow and more disgusted with his plastic lifestyle than he'd ever been, even at his lowest moments.

"Sorry I barked at you."

"Don't worry about it," she replied, shrugging off his apology. "Try the mousse. It's fantastic."

He looked up as she spooned another bite into her mouth and closed her eyes in sybaritic pleasure. The pink tip of her tongue appeared again and captured a smidgen of chocolate from her upper lip. Drawing a deep breath, he carefully replaced his spoon and reached for his water, downing half a glassful.

As Beth swallowed the last spoonful, she noticed Justin had barely touched his own dessert. Her questioning eyes met his fiery gaze and she shivered from what felt like a physical touch. His unleashed energy seemed to swirl around him like an invisible force, sucking her toward him.

"Coffee?" he suggested.

Beth shook her head, as much to sweep away her imaginings as to answer him. "I'd better be going. I have to get up early tomorrow."

He glanced at the gold Rolex. "I'll drive you. I don't have to be at the airport until morning."

Meaning what? His heated gaze conjured images that disturbed what little peace of mind she had left. It definitely was time to go home. Alone. Besides, what about Melanie?

"I don't want you falling asleep at the wheel," he added.

Beth stared at her empty plate. "I'll sleep at Marlene's penthouse tonight and go home in the morning."

"Then I'll see you to your car."

As they left the restaurant and stepped onto the escalator, a lively jazz tune drifted upward from the lobby. Beth caught herself tapping on the rail to the beat of the music. As they crossed the lobby, she was tempted to linger for a while to listen to the band. Then she spotted Bob Greeno strategically stationed behind a huge potted palm. He recognized them immediately. At least he recognized Justin—Beth wasn't the celebrity. Before the seedy little man could accost them, though, a security guard ambled by, and Greeno scooted back out of sight.

Beth frowned and hurried through the revolving door, with Justin close behind her. They waited for the Jaguar to arrive, both occupied with their own thoughts. Though they didn't touch, Beth could feel the heat of his presence at her side. Uncomfortable with the silence, she finally spoke.

"Well, thanks, I think. It's been an interesting experience." *That sounded stupid.* "I mean—"

Justin's fingers on her lips stopped her for the second time that day. The car arrived, but Beth barely noticed as the tingle traveled from her lips to the tips of her toes. "Don't say anything. You don't need to," he said.

Beth nodded and reached for the car door. His hand covered hers on the handle. Justin opened his mouth as if to speak, then closed it. He nudged her aside and jerked open the door.

"Get in," he ordered, all softness gone. When she didn't comply, he repeated the order. "Hurry! Greeno's coming through the door."

Beth needed no further urging. She slid behind the wheel, stepped on the clutch, and turned the key. She reached for the door handle and encountered Justin's knee instead.

"Move over."

Though confused at his command, she scooted when she saw he intended to get behind the wheel whether she moved or not. She scrambled over the gear box and flopped into the leather passenger seat as Greeno reached the car. Ignoring the rapping at the window, she turned to Justin and tugged at the swath of green silk that had trailed behind her and now was lodged firmly beneath Justin's rear.

"Nice legs," Justin commented, then stepped hard on the gas pedal.

The fabric pulled free as the car jerked into motion and spun out of the hotel drive onto the street in a squeal of complaining tires. Beth fell hard against the door and cursed.

"Hang on," Justin warned. Beth's only answer was to snap the seat belt into place and shut her eyes tightly. After three sharp turns, the Jaguar halted and Justin cut the engine.

Beth opened her eyes, but didn't recognize anything at first. Then she saw the outline of the downtown skyline in front of her. Looking around, she quickly got her bearings. They were in a half-vacant parking lot a couple of blocks from the hotel. The bright streetlights cast eerie shadows across the car's interior, but the area was well lit enough to be fairly safe.

"What was that all about?" Beth asked.

"Bob Greeno. I didn't want what I have to say to you on the front page of the supermarket tabloids."

"Good-bye is hardly incriminating. Or even embarrassing."

His touch trailed electric fire up her arm, burning through the thin silk. "That's not what I had in mind," he whispered, leaning closer still until his hands cupped her face.

"Oh?" was all she could manage, and even that emerged as a bare whisper as his lips brushed hers in a soft caress until she melted against the seat.

He kissed her with a practiced urgency, a heady mix of experience and barely controlled passion that unleashed unfamiliar emotions. At last he lifted his head, but Beth's lips clung to his, making retreat impossible. His thumb stroked a path of fire on the nape of her neck, and that path was somehow connected to her lungs, tightening the band across her chest until she could scarcely draw a breath. She wasn't conscious that her hands had slipped under his shirt until he groaned and pulled them away, capturing them with his own.

Then he slowly kissed each finger, one by one, until Beth groaned herself. She shifted and tucked her head against his shoulder while his arms closed about her, wrapping her close within his warmth. They stayed that way for a while, Beth didn't know how long. Then they eased apart, finally noticing the awkwardness imposed by bucket seats and the hard, bumpy gear box.

He touched her cheek, and a swelling happiness surged through Beth. It made no sense, this giddy feeling. It simply existed. She knew that tomorrow she'd feel like an idiot, but she pushed that thought away. Tomorrow was soon enough for regrets and second thoughts.

"I should go," Justin murmured, yet showed no sign of leaving. "Don't forget me."

Beth had to laugh at that. "Maybe if I finish in the fields early enough I'll watch your show Tuesday night with Charley and Aunt Eva."

"Do that." He unlatched the door and the overhead light came on. His eyes were still smoky with desire. "One more thing. I'm glad it was you tonight and not one of those hard-nosed career types."

Beth straightened in her seat. "Produce farming is a career and I'm damned serious about it. If I wasn't, I'd have sold the place or gone bankrupt by now."

Justin groaned. "Open mouth. Insert foot. I meant that you're very real, very warm and very different from the women I've dated, in my personal life and on these publicity tours."

Beth's jaw dropped. "You've done other auctions?"

"Three. They were awful." His expression was so grim that Beth couldn't help but laugh.

"It's terrible being a sex symbol, isn't it."

"It's terrible having to go back to California now," he replied, throwing Beth off balance just as she was regaining her equilibrium. "I want to see more of you. I wish I could stay another day or two. Maybe I can come back."

Beth's smile was tinged with sadness. "You won't. Your life is busy and filled with people like you. Tonight was no big deal, just another publicity appearance with a few crazies thrown in to keep you from getting bored."

"Stay here tonight." A faint tremor traveled from his finger to her lips, then through her body to her knees. Naked desire flashed in his eyes before he masked it.

Beth drew a shaky breath. She didn't doubt his sincerity now. No one could act that well. He couldn't conjure up that combination of trembling hands, fiery eyes, and husky voice. He couldn't make the pulse point at his throat throb on command, could he?

"What about Melanie?" She asked the question aloud this time. They both needed the reminder.

"What about her? She isn't my keeper, and I'm not hers."

"You two seem close." She struggled to put her intuitive perceptions into words. "Like you've known each other for years. You talk without saying a word. And I suspect that this problem that's cropped up is more Melanie's problem than yours, yet you're there for her to lean on."

"Of course I am. What kind of brother would I be if I wasn't."

"Your *sister*," she said dumbly. She'd completely misread the meaning of the familiar touching, the speaking glances. She felt like a fool.

"You thought—"

"Never mind what I thought," she interrupted. "It's too embarrassing. Now I'd better be going. I have work to do. And this really isn't my style." Suddenly she realized that the dome light spotlighted them, creating a live show for passersby and eyes shielded by the shades and curtains of the surrounding buildings. She waited for him to get out of the car, but he didn't move.

"I'll be back." His tone was a promise, making her forget anyone might be watching.

"Why?" she asked, genuinely puzzled by his sincerity.

"Damned if I know. You're everything I've been running away from since I left that little Illinois town twelve years ago." With that said, he planted a final, hard kiss on her lips and left the car, locking the door before he closed it. "I'll call you," he added.

She'd heard that line before. "You don't have the number," she couldn't resist reminding him.

"I copied it from the phone dial in the shed," he answered, tapping his breast pocket. "It's right here." He winked, then took to his heels.

Beth sat there in the passenger seat for a moment, then realized he was watching her from the corner. At first she thought he'd decided to return, then she realized he had waited to see that she was safely on her way.

A warm, protected feeling stole over her as she scrambled back into the driver's seat and started the car. She waved from the parking lot exit, then sped up the street toward the penthouse.

By the next morning, she was more confused than ever. She'd spent half the night reliving those moments in the car, only to fall asleep and dream about them. All her mental meanderings boiled down to one simple question. No, three. Why her? And was he sincere, or had she been taken in by an actor's skill? And what had he meant by his parting words, that she was everything he had been running from? Not so simple, after all.

Two days passed without a word from Justin. By then she'd decided she'd been a fool to think he might find her more than a very temporary amusement, no matter what he'd said. Though it still made her angry to remember how she'd melted in his arms. Angry, humiliated, and desperately afraid she'd become another amusing story in the life of TV and film star Justin Kyle. A proverbial notch in the belt, she thought, then smiled to herself. Hardly that. She'd spent a few hours in the man's company and kissed him like a demon. Exciting as it had been, it hardly constituted abandoned, passionate sex. She'd lost nothing but her pride.

Something happened on Saturday, however, that pushed Justin Kyle temporarily to the back of her mind. The chef of her largest client, The Choutou Grill, called at dinnertime, and after a string of blue language, the chef informed Beth that he'd found a more reliable source for the tender salad crops she'd supplied.

"How can you say Thompson Farm is unreliable?" she asked, when she could finally get a word in edgewise. "For six months we've supplied you and there's never been a complaint until now."

"Yesterday afternoon, I canceled the tomatoes—we had too many left yet. And I ordered extra buttercrunch and cilantro. I get a piddling amount of buttercrunch and no cilantro so I have to go down to the grocery store and buy dried flakes of cilantro. You know what this does to the sauces?"

"Who did you speak to?" She didn't dare mention yet that the cilantro was a victim of Witch's double rampage.

"I don't know. Some kid. He say he write it down in the book," the chef said.

"I'll get to the bottom of this, and I assure you that it won't happen again," Beth cajoled. "I'll throw in a week's supply of basil, free of charge as compensation."

"No compensation. No more deliveries. Wilson Brothers have my business now." Click.

"Great," she muttered, then headed for the produce

shed, bellowing out Charley's name. However, Charley swore he'd written the message down.

"Didn't you check the book before you packed the truck?" he asked her.

"Of course. There was no order from The Choutou."

"You missed it," he said, snatching up the notebook that hung from a string by the telephone extension. He flipped through the pages, front to back twice. "It ain't there."

"No, it ain't," she mimicked. "Are you sure you put it in the book and not on the back of an envelope or something?"

Charley waved his arms around. "You see any paper lying around out here? Maybe I wrote it on a lettuce leaf and the slugs ate it last night."

"Charley, I—"

"It was right here. See, this page is torn out."

"Well, who would do that?" The question remained unanswered, because none of the employees claimed the blame, and by Monday it was business as usual, except the delivery route was a bit shorter. And if Beth still jumped every time the phone rang, no one mentioned it.

But by the end of the next week, Beth had stopped getting excited every time she heard the telephone. She'd put the entire auction incident into perspective, and had even gone to a Tuesday-night movie with the veterinarian who treated her animals. He hadn't been in the area long, but the young widower's easygoing nature and his tall, lanky body and bony features were appealing in a lost-dog sort of way.

Ross Dixon didn't set her senses on fire when he kissed her, but theirs was an easy friendship built on common interests. The rumor was that his wife had died in a farm accident several years ago. But he'd never mentioned her when he'd been with Beth. They talked about farming, animals, and little else. He was from her world, and not likely to leave it. Ross was no Justin Kyle, and for that Beth was grateful.

So she was more than surprised late in the week when she returned from an evening horseback ride around the farm and found the message taped on the back door. "Gone to town with Charley. Dinner in oven. Call Justin," Aunt Eva's spidery script stated. A phone number was scribbled at the bottom of the paper.

Call Justin! Excitement warred with irritation that he'd waited so long to contact her. She hesitated, then went to the phone and picked up the receiver. Her finger hovered over the rotary dial, then lifted as she dropped the receiver back into its cradle. Not now. She was too tired to talk. She'd take a shower and eat dinner. Then maybe she'd call. She realized she was stalling, but the realization didn't make it any easier to dial that number.

She'd just stepped out of the shower when the phone rang. She wrapped a towel around herself and hurried down the stairs. She snatched up the receiver on the seventh ring.

"Beth?" Justin's voice awakened all the feelings from the kiss in the Jaguar. Goose bumps dimpled her damp flesh even though it was quite warm there in the hall.

"Yes?" She cleared her throat, hating the breathy quality that revealed too much of what she was feeling. "It's me. I was going to call you back in a little while."

"Is this a bad time?"

She glanced down at the puddle forming on the polished wood floor and reached for a throw rug to soak up the water. "No. I can talk now," she said.

"The paper I wrote your number on has some notes on the back, printed sideways like someone was in a hurry. Something about Choutou and cilantro? Is that important? I thought I had a clean page, but this was on the back."

"Damn!" Beth muttered. "It was *you*."

"Was it important?"

"It was an order change. The client canceled."

"Oh, then everything's all right then."

"No. I mean canceled permanently. He found another supplier." Beth's tone conveyed the seriousness of the situation.

"How important was this client?"

"Very. Not to mention the fact that he has a big mouth. He can really hurt us."

Justin was silent for a moment. "I'm sorry. I didn't even find the message until this morning."

Beth sighed. "These things happen. I suspect the man was just looking for an excuse. He's gone to Wilson Brothers, and their prices are lower."

"Can you cut yours to compete?"

"Not really. Not and consistently deliver top-quality produce."

"Sorry I didn't try to call sooner. Maybe I'd have found the message. But between Melanie's problems and this new movie, I haven't had a moment to spare."

"What movie?" she asked, wisely steering away from what clearly was none of her business.

"It's a lead role in *Nebraska Sunset*." He spoke quickly now, his excitement obvious, even through the low buzz of static on the line.

"Never heard of it," she said as she adjusted the slipping towel. "What's it about?"

"Old farmer dies, leaving the land jointly to his sons. One wants to sell out, the other wants to keep it. Sounds like another Heartland sob story, but this one's really different. It's a terrific script."

"It doesn't sound like your type of film," she said, recalling the adventure flicks he'd played in, not to mention "Vice Cops." "Trying to change your image?"

"Something like that. Anyway, I wondered if you could help me research the role."

"This isn't Nebraska," she pointed out. "Hey, I thought the script was already written. What could you need to research?"

"I want to work on your farm for a few weeks to get a handle on the character—how he feels and the situations he faces. I'd pay you a consultant's fee."

"Why here? Why not closer to home? Last I heard, there were loads of farmers left in California."

"California isn't like the Midwest. Different climate. Different crops and problems."

"Are you suggesting this because you feel guilty about the message?" she asked.

"I'd like to make that up to you, but that's not why I want to work for you. I really do need to do this research."

Beth was silent for a moment. Her immediate impulse was to agree, but then she remembered how smooth Justin's palms were and how much chaos had accompanied his first visit to the farm. She remembered how much chaos he'd created in her mind in one evening. To work with him, side by side, day after day, would be madness.

"I don't think I can help you," she finally murmured.

"You don't want to see me again?" He sounded hurt.

"It's not that," she said, though that was exactly the problem. She didn't dare for fear she'd turn into one of his goggling fans, a slobbering statistic. "I'm short-staffed as it is. I can't spare anybody to take you around and explain how things work. Besides, this is probably the wrong kind of farm anyway. I grow organic produce, remember?"

"There's a fat consulting fee in this for you," he pointed out. "I've put your place in as a possible filming site. And the publicity from this would help your business, too. It could put you on the map."

Beth thought about that. It took all of five seconds for her fury to erupt. Of all the arrogant donkeys Marlene had set her up with, Justin was the worst, she thought, forgetting the goose pimples she'd felt only moments before. "I can't be bought," she said in a voice that would have chilled molten lava. "Furthermore, I don't need a bunch of Hollywood know-it-alls trampling the lettuce and running sound booms or whatever it is they use through the greenhouse wall."

Justin's sigh was audible across the miles. "Don't be a fool, Beth. You could make a lot of repairs around the place with the money this kind of deal could bring."

"We're doing just fine, thank you."

"Come on. The house hasn't been painted in twenty years, I'd bet. The barn roof sags and half your fenceposts are rotten," he said.

The fact that he was right didn't change Beth's mind. It only infuriated her that he'd taken it upon himself to solve her obvious financial problems without consulting her to see whether his idea was acceptable. And it wasn't, not by a long shot. She'd built a good life for herself here, and she was proud of the progress she'd made in the last few years. The farm had come a long way from the overgrown, tumbledown wreck she'd inherited. It wasn't in peak condition yet, but it was getting there.

She'd succeed or fail on her own merits, because in the end, that's all she could depend on. She'd learned that lesson at the age of five when her father walked out and never came back.

"Beth? Beth, are you there?" His voice penetrated her thoughts.

"The answer is no." She hung up.

He called right back. "Don't hang up," he ordered before she'd even had a chance to say hello.

"Beth, it's not just the movie. I want to see you again. That night, I felt things I'd never even imagined. I know you felt something, too."

Beth couldn't deny it. She couldn't lie that well. So she said nothing.

"I'm right, aren't I?"

"We're adults," she answered. "That means we don't have to act on physical attractions. I like my life the way it is. I don't have a lot of spare time, and I don't have a lot of money. My goals aren't that lofty. But they're *my* goals and I'm not giving them up, not even temporarily."

"Give me one day."

Beth hesitated. Was she making a snap judgment she'd regret? He meant well, but those good intentions could undermine her carefully guarded independence. She'd grown up watching Marlene run through a string of men who promised to take her away from it all or make her life better. Alfred had been the only one to make good on that promise. Even so, Marlene had nothing without him.

"I don't know," she answered. "I'll have to think about it." And she slowly replaced the receiver.

She half expected him to call back again, but he didn't, not that night or the next two nights. He was letting her think. Or maybe he'd decided it wasn't worth the trouble. If that was the case, her first impulse had been right. She had no use for a man who gave up easily. Those were the kind who left when life got tougher than they were instead of sticking around and toughening themselves up.

She was still thinking about it Saturday morning when she and Charley strolled along the dam of the small lake that supplied most of the water for irrigating the gardens during the peak of summer. The spring rains had been heavy, and the run-off water flooding over the top of the dam had weakened it. Edgar squawked as he zoomed between them then landed on Beth's shoulder, but she brushed him away and turned to Charley.

"I guess we'll have to get Ted out here with the bulldozer," she said, mentally calculating the damage to the already tight budget. If she put off painting the house for another year, and if the truck engine held out, she could manage the expense. Just barely. Maybe she should take Justin up on his proposal.

Charley rubbed his whiskered chin. "Naw. I think I can do it with the tractor and the snow blade."

Beth frowned and walked down the sloped embankment. "I don't know, Charley. The tractor's not made for excavating. Neither is the snow blade."

"I can do a temporary job, enough to hold the dam through the summer and fall until we get the feed corn in. You'll have enough cash then to pay for the dozer job," Charley reasoned.

It made sense, and in the end, Beth consented. She wondered guiltily how much her reluctance to fall in with Justin's plan had to do with her decision. The next day she listened carefully to the sound of the tractor as it strained and pushed and pulled, moving the dirt into place and packing it beneath the heavy tires. At lunch, Charley proclaimed the job nearly finished.

"Just have some touch-up work near the top. Come on out and have a look after the vet leaves," he added, and harrumphed at Beth and Aunt Eva's warnings about caution.

The vet, Ross Dixon, arrived as Beth and Charley were returning to work. Charley climbed aboard the tractor and headed out to the lake, while Beth led Ross to the barn. Witch had gotten out again that morning, and when Beth found her, she was tangled in barbed wire.

The cow limped heavily when Beth led her out of the stall and tied her to a post. "I cleaned the cuts out, but a couple don't look right," she said.

Ross nodded and moved in for a closer examination, then dodged a kick. "Nothing a few stitches and a shot of antibiotics won't cure," he said. "I think we'd better start with a sedative, though."

As the two of them worked with the cow, Edgar perched on a nearby post and mimicked Beth's soft croonings. Through the raucous sound, Beth tracked the tractor's movements with her ears, just as she had all morning.

Suddenly the steady rumble changed to a racing roar. Then it sputtered and died completely. Beth's eyes met Ross's. Leaving Witch tied, they took off at a dead run for the lake. Ross's legs were longer, but fear lent Beth speed. She reached the dam ten paces ahead of Ross. What she saw there was worse than she had imagined. Charley lay motionless on the embankment, pinned beneath the overturned tractor.

"Careful," Ross warned as he scrambled down behind her. "The tractor might roll again.

Charley's face was a pasty gray, but Ross found a faint, if somewhat irregular, pulse.

"His leg's pinned," Beth muttered, and started up the embankment.

"Wait," Ross called.

She turned in midstride, stumbling slightly. "I'm going for help."

Ross glanced down at Charley again, then back at Beth. "Tell the ambulance crew he may have had a heart attack," he said.

Beth's world spun around, then righted itself as she quelled the panic before it could take hold. "Right," she answered, then ran for all she was worth. Robby, one of the high school boys, met her at the gate. She gave him the pertinent details between gasps and sent him on to the house to telephone for an ambulance. The other two boys caught up with her as she reached the old pickup truck.

She drove the truck through the field as fast as she dared, then positioned it at the top of the embankment. With the boys' help, she and Ross secured the tractor with the truck's winch. Then they used it to raise the tractor just enough to carefully pull Charley free. Everything after that passed in a blur, the ambulance ride, the interminable wait at the hospital until the doctor appeared with news of Charley's condition.

He reassured Beth and Aunt Eva that Charley would

live, though he warned that the recovery would be lengthy. "It was a mild heart attack, but he'll have to make some changes. It's his knee that worries me, though. It's pretty badly damaged. He'll have to have surgery. Right now, he's awake and not very cooperative."

"He's awake?" Beth felt a weight leave her shoulders.

The doctor drew a deep breath and rolled his eyes. "He's demanding to be released."

"He'll make it, the old coot," Aunt Eva muttered waspishly, but her eyes glittered with unshed tears.

"Can I talk to him?" Beth asked.

"I wish you would," the doctor said, and escorted her to the intensive-care ward of the small county hospital. He motioned to the nurse to leave, then followed her out of the room, leaving Beth alone with her old friend.

He looked frail lying there against the stark-white sheets and attached to a myriad of tubes. "You really did it this time, Charley," she chastised him, and was rewarded with a pained grin.

"They say I can't go home."

"You can't walk."

He grimaced. "Knee hurts like hell. Bad hip. Bad knee. Bad heart. Might as well just die."

Beth took his hand and squeezed, communicating her fear. She'd heard somewhere that the will to live was half the battle. "You don't mean that," she said.

"Course not," he answered. "The important parts still work fine. Head. Hands. Unmentionables." He winked.

Beth couldn't have stopped the grin even if she'd wanted to. "Maybe when they fix that knee, you can talk them into working on the hip, too."

"Hmmmph."

"You'll sign the permission papers?"

He grimaced. "Yeah, if you'll stop nagging."

"Deal," she said, and bent to kiss his pale cheek. She squeezed his hand, then pulled away. "I'll send in Aunt Eva."

The older woman was waiting just outside in the corridor.

"Full of spit and vinegar, is he?" Aunt Eva said.

"Same old Charley. He's expecting you." Beth nudged her aunt toward Charley's door, but the woman hung back, shaking her head.

"I need to tell you something first," she insisted.

"Whatever it is, it can wait."

Aunt Eva glanced at the nurse hovering nearby. "No, it can't," she insisted and drew Beth aside. "It's about the insurance."

Beth frowned. "It's a good thing we kept the policy up. I just hope it covers everything."

"It won't."

"Well, most of it," Beth answered. "It's a good policy. That's why it's so expensive."

Aunt Eva bit her lip, then clasped Beth's arms. "I let the policy lapse," she said in a rush.

Beth felt herself blanche. "You what?"

"Last winter when the transmission went out on the truck, I used the money for the insurance to pay the mechanic. I figured I'd make it up somewhere else, that we'd only have to go a month or so, but there never seemed to be any extra money."

The older woman appeared shrunken by the double blow of Charley's injury and her well-meaning shuffling of the farm's funds. Angry as Beth was, she couldn't be so cruel as to berate the woman for doing what she thought best. If only Aunt Eva had told her, though. She could have managed something. It was Beth's own fault, really, for not taking responsibility for her own bookkeeping, or even paying close enough attention to know how serious their financial problems were.

Beth pulled Aunt Eva into a hug. "Don't worry about it," she said. "I'll take care of everything. There's always workmen's compensation." She tried to sound confident, but inside she was terrified.

Aunt Eva shook her head. "I doubt they'd pay a dime. He's not really on our list of employees. We've been paying him in cash like he asked. I thought you knew."

Beth didn't, and the implications disturbed her. Had they paid any taxes on his behalf? The specter of an Internal Revenue Service audit rose in her mind. There was nothing she could change about the situation at the moment, but she was going to take a close look at the books as soon as she got home.

"Go on and see Charley," she urged.

As the door closed behind the older woman, the nurse approached Beth. "Are you his daughter?"

"No, his employer." It sounded so formal, nothing like the relationship they really had. "He doesn't have any family. Just us."

"Maybe you could help with the insurance papers."

"He doesn't have any insurance."

"Then you'll have to go down the hall to the business office and make arrangements for payment," she said, smiling reassuringly. "Don't worry. It's only a formality."

But it wasn't, Beth thought later after a long, honest talk with the hospital business manager. Charley's recovery would be lengthy, and very expensive. The hospital official couldn't say exactly how much it would cost, but his rough estimates had brought a gasp to Beth's lips. She didn't have that kind of money, and Charley surely didn't.

She drove home alone since Aunt Eva refused to leave the hospital. Although Beth planned to return later that evening, just now, there were things she must do. By the time she reached home, the tractor was parked back beside the barn with the truck, and the cable was neatly wound on the winch. The boys were back in the gardens, and Ross was gone. Edgar greeted her with a loud chortle and swooped on to her shoulder. Instead of chasing him away, she pulled on a pair of work gloves and coaxed him into riding on her hand.

Remembering Witch, Beth headed for the cow's stall. Ross had finished dressing the wounds and someone had thought to feed her and the other animals, Beth noticed. As she watched Witch placidly chew the hay, the tears she'd been holding all afternoon escaped and streamed down her face.

She deposited Edgar on a post, then climbed into the stall occupied by her old mare, Brownie. The horse was a friend from the days when life was less complicated, when Grandma was there to solve all her problems. An old friend, like Charley was. She wrapped her arms around Brownie's neck, then closed her eyes and tried to remember a time when Charley hadn't been a part of Thompson Farm. She couldn't. He was as much a part of the place as Beth, Aunt Eva, Edgar, Brownie, and even that crazy cow.

Later, as her tears dried, her thoughts turned to the mounting bills, not just the hospital bills, but the mortgage and outstanding loans on the new greenhouse and this year's planting costs. How would they pay for it all? She mentally reviewed what she knew of the accounts, but she wasn't sure how bad the situation was. It had been months since she'd had time to go over them with Aunt Eva. She hoped the two hospitals would be willing to set up a payment schedule. A very long-term one. Then she remembered that there was an alternative.

She swallowed her reservations and convinced herself it was the only reasonable path. Asking her stepfather for money was out of the question. She couldn't do it, not when she was trying to build her own niche. It wouldn't be the same if Alfred helped buy it for her. But she could earn the money by helping a certain actor prepare for a new role.

She strode determinedly toward the house before she could change her mind or lose her courage. She searched through the trash until she found the slip of paper with Justin's number on it, then picked up the phone and dialed.

FOUR

Justin's phone rang twice, then a third time before a crisp, female voice answered.

Beth hesitated, tempted to replace the receiver quietly and forget about it. But her financial problems wouldn't simply go away. "I need to speak to Mr. Kyle," she finally said.

"He isn't here now. This is his housekeeper. Your message?"

"It's personal."

"Of course." The two words were laced with a long-suffering sneer. "And your business?"

Beth sighed, then forced herself to maintain a pleasant tone, no matter how disagreeable the other woman insisted on being. "A consulting job he mentioned."

"That's a new one," the voice muttered. Beth rolled her eyes toward the ceiling, wondering if Justin would ever see her message. Obviously the woman assumed Beth was a fan who had somehow gotten Justin's telephone number. "Anything else?" the housekeeper added.

"Yes, tell him the baby is doing fine. And I'm really

sorry about what the dog did in his car," she said, quickly adding her name and telephone number, then hanging up. There, she thought, staring at the old black phone. That should give the woman something to think about. For a moment, Beth debated whether to wait around to see if he called or to return to the hospital to see Charley and perhaps persuade Aunt Eva to come home. The hospital won hands down. She'd never sat by the phone before. That's what answering machines were for. Besides, she figured the chances were fifty-fifty that her message didn't make it past the dragon lady. And if it didn't she'd just figure out something else.

As she headed upstairs for a shower, the phone rang and Beth hurried back down and snatched up the receiver.

"Can we start in two weeks?" Justin asked immediately, not bothering with a simple courtesy like "hello." His enthusiasm only irritated Beth's overstrung nerves as he continued. "We should wrap up this episode by tomorrow. I have a few loose ends to tie up, but I'll be free by Tuesday."

"I haven't agreed yet," she reminded him as soon as she could get a word in edgewise.

"Of course you have. You called."

Beth took a deep breath, and counted to ten. She couldn't afford to let her temper erupt and ruin the best chance she had of raising some quick cash. When she spoke, her voice was controlled, with only a hint of the trembling anger that threatened. "I need to know a few things, such as how much money is involved." There, she'd said it.

"Blunt, aren't you," Justin answered, sounding

amused. Then his tone turned serious, almost stern. "You aren't having financial problems, are you?"

The knot in Beth's stomach tightened. She cleared her throat and strove for a normal, nonchalant answer. She almost succeeded. "Nothing serious. Everything will be fine once the field crops are harvested," she said.

"But you could use the money now," he prompted. "How much?"

"How much does the job pay?"

"I'm not sure. Someone from the studio will call you to work out the contract details for filming, assuming, of course, that they choose your farm and not one of the others they're checking out. As for our arrangement—"

"No filming," Beth interrupted.

"You'd make more money that way. You could rebuild the place and have money left over. You ought to consider it."

"Only as a last resort," she said.

He paused. "Then it's just between you and me." He made it sound like a challenge.

"How much does the studio allow for things like this?"

"Your fee will come out of the money I make on the movie, same as if I hired a voice coach or took a class."

Beth digested that. Taking advantage of her silence, Justin continued. "As I said, I could be there in two weeks. We could spend the first couple of days going over the daily routine. You could take me around the farm and such, then we could come up with a schedule so that I get a good sampling of the types of situations

I'd run into if I really were a farmer. You know, equipment breakdowns and so on.''

"You want me to break something so you can fix it?" Beth's uneasy knot twisted and pulled tighter.

"Well, not exactly. I want to know what it's really like to be a farmer. To experience it.''

Beth shook her head, then remembered he couldn't see her. "You can't just create the experience. It just happens. Either you figure out what makes a farmer ticks or you don't. Some people never do." *Marlene, for instance.*

"Let's give it a shot," he said. "What could it hurt?"

Me. The unbidden thought sent a shiver down her spine before she stiffened it. "I don't think this is going to work," she said, telling herself he'd be more hindrance than help.

"Of course it will. It has to. I don't know any other farmers in the hinterland. And I can't do it out here. My face is too well known. The sleaze press would find me in less than a week. But your place will be perfect. I know it. It just takes a little planning, a little coordination." His cajoling tone grated her the wrong way. "Besides, I feel guilty for making you lose an important account. I'd like to make it up to you.''

"Are you sure you're up to this—physically, I mean?" she asked, remembering his well-cared-for hands and smooth palms. He obviously hadn't done much physical labor lately.

He snorted. "How hard can it be to plant turnips and tomatoes and chase a black cow around?"

How hard, indeed, Beth thought, thinking of the nights she'd fallen into bed, too exhausted to even undress, and of the uncontrollable droughts and storms that could ruin a season's work. Well, he'd asked for it. She was beginning to think she might enjoy showing him what farm life really was. He deserved a set-down.

"Suppose I agree, how long would you be here?" she asked with deceptive meekness.

"I figured on about twelve weeks. How does that sound to you? And I want to stay in the house, too. It'll be hard to get a feel for the part if I stay in a motel and eat room-service."

Beth almost laughed at the idea of the tiny Shady Side Motel offering room service. Guests were lucky if they got clean sheets, from what she'd heard. But the thought of Justin Kyle sleeping just down the hallway from her was more disturbing than funny.

"And you couldn't tell anyone I was there," he continued.

Beth straightened. "Why?" she asked. "I doubt Bob Greeno and his kind will expect to find someone like you working on a farm."

His amusement vibrated through the miles, deepening the timbre of his voice. "What's that supposed to mean?"

"You have hands like an accountant. Soft and smooth. You'll be blistered within an hour after you get here. And for a Californian, you're pretty pale. You'll sunburn."

"They'll toughen up. I had to wear gloves for four months to get rid of the calluses for a documentary I did on Mozart. I also had to stay out of the sun," he said, then added with a snooty accent, "I played the king, and kings don't labor in the sun."

"How interesting," she said in a tone that implied it wasn't. "Well, don't worry. I don't plan to take out a newspaper ad, but people are going to want to know who the new farmhand is.''

''I'll be there to work, not sign autographs.''

''I think being a celebrity has gone to your head,'' she grated out.

''You just don't realize what a market there is for celebrity photos and tidbits of information. Reporters like that Bob Greeno don't believe I'm entitled to a shred of privacy. I've had to take extra security measures since I've been on 'Vice Cops.' Living your life out there in the country, you haven't had to deal with those kinds of things much.''

''I'm not a complete hick,'' she retorted.

His sigh caressed her ear, but she was in no mood for stroking. ''Sorry,'' he said. ''I didn't realize I'd insulted you. I just meant that I've had to be more security conscious. It's just a necessary evil.''

''Oh. Well, the security will cost more,'' Beth said with biting sarcasm, her rising temper loosening her control over her tongue.

''What's your bottom line?'' he asked.

Beth named a price equal to the estimate the hospital administrator had made of Charley's upcoming medical bills.

''Are you kidding?''

Beth pursed her lips. ''That's my price.'' Start high and negotiate down. That's what Charley had taught her.

''Does that include bed and board?'' His silky tone skittered from her ear to her spine and down the length of it. She'd intended to negotiate the price, not the services.

''Whose bed?'' she demanded in a slightly husky tone.

"I'd prefer yours, but I don't suppose that's included in the deal."

"Damned right."

"It should be. That's more than my father made the year I left for college."

"Look, mister. I have bills to pay and a business to run. That's the price I'll do the job for. Take it or leave it." She slammed down the receiver. Ten seconds later, it rang.

"Well," she barked into the receiver.

"Beth?"

Through the haze of anger, Beth recognized Aunt Eva's voice. "I'm sorry," she said. "What is it? Is Charley—"

"He's asleep," Aunt Eva said. "I just wanted to tell you so you wouldn't waste a trip into town. Mrs. Thomas offered me her guest room for a couple of days when she and the reverend were at the hospital a bit ago. You'll have to manage without me, just until Charley's in better shape. Don't bother with the cleaning. I'll just have to do it over again anyway. And if you need help with the books, bring them in. I can always do that here at the hospital."

"Of course," Beth said, more relieved than offended. "I'll see you sometime tomorrow, then."

"Whenever you can break free. I'm sure Charley will enjoy your company."

"Aunt Eva? I've been thinking about getting some of those study guides for the high school equivalency test. Maybe while I'm in town I could see when the test will be given."

"That's a good idea," her aunt replied. "You need your diploma. Charley and I, we're getting old. We won't always be here to help you."

"I know," Beth murmured. "Take care of him, and yourself. I want you both around for a while yet."

The phone rang again as soon as she replaced the receiver. She was tempted not to answer, but was afraid it would be Aunt Eva again, or even the hospital.

"Thompson Farm," she said into the receiver.

"Done," Justin sliced out. "I'll see you a week from Tuesday." The line went dead before she could reply. Feeling suddenly weak in the knees, she leaned back against the wall and sank to the floor. She couldn't believe the gamble she'd taken. Stupidly, she'd let her temper get the best of her when she should have been begging for the job at any price. Yet he'd agreed. And for the life of her, she couldn't figure out why.

Unless he wanted to pick up where they'd left off that night in the Jaguar. And that was something Beth couldn't do. She wouldn't be Justin Kyle's summer plaything. She wouldn't be anyone's plaything. If and when she gave her heart—and made love—it would be to a man who lived in her world, not someone who was just visiting.

The problem was, just the thought of him heated her blood. She wasn't sure she was ready to test her resolve or her grandmother's firm, old-fashioned teachings against an attraction that strong.

What have I gotten myself into?

Justin told himself he was ten times a fool as he backed his late-model Jeep out of the garage and pointed it east, away from the California coast. He repeated it twice an hour until he reached the Rockies and left the highway for the back roads that led to a friend's mountain cabin. Then the sheer grandeur of the towering expanses of bare rock rising above the treed plateaus carried his thoughts beyond himself and instinct took over.

And his instincts told him that his first impression of Beth Thompson had been the right one. The report from the private investigator he'd hired only confirmed that, and he felt guilty now that he'd ever suspected her motives or had her investigated.

But the fee she'd demanded was high, more the bid of a savvy insider than a midwestern farm girl. Blame it on the company he'd been keeping, or the parade of willing, desirable bodies thrown his way by grasping females in recent years. But for a while he'd suspected she was offering, and expecting, more than consulting services.

He didn't know when it had happened, when he'd realized that he could no longer tell whether the woman in his bed wanted *him* or the things he could provide. Sometimes it was his money or what it could buy, but more often it was the veneer of success that they seemed to think might rub off on them. To see and be seen, with the right people in the right place, by the right people at the right place. It wasn't his life. Not really. And he wondered how much longer he could tolerate it.

By the time he reached the turnoff to the cabin, he realized that what irritated him most was the fact that he couldn't just forget about her. His main purpose for going to Missouri wasn't the research. He told himself repeatedly that he'd inadvertently harmed her business by holding on to that message, and this was the only way he could make it up to her. He could replace the farm's lost income with this consulting job. But the fact was, she'd gotten under his skin so quickly and so deeply that he'd have met her price anyway just to let this obsession of his play itself out. And obsessions were dangerous.

Two days of solitude at the cabin chased away the tenseness he'd carried with him from California, but not his desire. If anything, it was stronger. But he was ready now, ready for the long drive to Missouri, ready to see whether Beth Ann Thompson was all he remembered.

He spent the last night just outside Kansas City in a cheap, chain motel. His four-day growth of beard and faded clothes made him blend right in with the truck drivers and factory workers at the diner where he ate an early breakfast. The anonymity appealed to him, and he decided to travel this way more often.

He reached the Thompson Farm drive long before the sun had dried the dew on the grass, and he breathed in the warm, earthy scents of morning. He felt good, better than he had in years. For twelve weeks, he would just be himself, Justin Schnell.

The moment the cherry-red Jeep pulled into the gravel space behind the house, Beth knew she'd made a mistake. The man who climbed out of the open door was Justin Kyle, all right. But he didn't look like the polished, pretty playboy who had arrived with Marlene. His shadowed and unshaven whiskers disguised his famous jawline, but he couldn't hide the mischievous glint in those gray-blue eyes. His faded jeans and crumpled "Save Our Planet" T-shirt looked like something one of her teenage employees would wear. And that was just the problem. He looked like he belonged there, right down to the well-worn watchband and scratched crystal. Only the Jeep seemed out of place.

An odd queasiness attacked her stomach, and she

wished she'd had something lighter than leftover chili for breakfast.

"Okay if I park here?" he called.

Beth stepped down off the porch and strode toward the bright vehicle. "Did you buy that thing because it was pretty or because you thought that's what a real farmer would drive?" she asked.

"No, I bought this because it has four-wheel drive and it handles well in sand and mud."

Beth eyed the Jeep dubiously. She'd be willing to bet that underneath the dust coating was a showroom-bright shine. "When?"

"Last year."

Beth raised her eyebrows, but didn't say a word.

"Really. Now if you'll show me where to put my things, I can unload this junk. Then we can go over the contract."

"I can't just now. I have an emergency order to fill."

Justin's brow furrowed. "What's up?"

"A new client, I hope. Their regular supplier didn't show up yesterday or today, so the manager called me. I have to move fast if I'm going to get this order together and into the city on time."

"This could replace the Choutou order?" he asked. "The one I screwed up for you?"

Beth didn't bother to deny that. He hadn't purposely stolen the message, but it was his fault it had gone missing. "This restaurant's bigger, though," she pointed out. "If I can get them to sign a contract, it'll more than make up for the Choutou cancellation."

"What can I do to help?"

Beth glanced around, and tapped restlessly, trying to decide where he could do the least damage. She didn't have time to answer questions just now, or show him around the farm. That would have to wait. "Take your stuff inside," she said. "Your room is upstairs at the end of the hall, the one with the blue quilt. Once you've unpacked, you can come down to the shed and watch us get this order ready." Without waiting to see whether he agreed, she turned and sprinted to the produce shed.

The next couple of hours passed in a flurry of activity as Beth and her crew rushed to fill the order. Everything was checked and double-checked, washed and rewashed to minimize the chances of any defects or insects slipping past their attention. She didn't need to explain how important this order was. They all knew it.

Beth had just carried the last basket of leaf lettuce into the produce shed when she collided with Justin beside one of the long wooden tables. "Ooops. Sorry," she murmured, and sidestepped.

"I'll take that," he said, grabbing it by the bottom and gently lowering it to the table. "Do I pack this like the others?" he called out, and Robby, one of the teenagers, answered in the affirmative.

Beth cast a puzzled glance his way, then watched as Justin straightened and repacked the tender lettuce into a delivery box. He moved swiftly, without a trace of awkwardness, gently tucking the individual bunches into place. "How long have you been down here?" she asked.

He shrugged. "A couple of hours, I guess. I figured this order was more important than unpacking."

"He's been a lot of help," Robby interjected as he passed them on the way to the truck with a load of radishes. Justin soon followed, and before long, Beth and Robby were ready to leave.

"What should I work on while you're gone?"

"A rain dance if you know one," Robby offered. "We had to turn the irrigation system on."

"Sorry, that's not part of my repertoire," Justin replied, grinning widely. "I'm more of a rock 'n' roll kind of guy."

Beth allowed a faint smile to crease her lips. "I don't suppose you'd consider relaxing and unpacking," she said.

"I guess I'll have to hunt up Charley and ask him what to do," Justin suggested.

Beth halted in her tracks. "I didn't tell you?"

"What? Did he quit?"

Beth combed her fingers through her tangled curls and quickly explained what had happened.

"He's lucky he's alive," Justin replied, stunned by the news.

"Yeah, he is," Beth agreed, then forced the huskiness from her voice. "Now, let's see. I guess you could weed the brassicas." Surely he couldn't do too much damage there, she thought. Any idiot could tell the difference between cabbage and chickweed.

"Brassicas?" He squinted in confusion.

"Cabbage, broccoli, cauliflower—that stuff," she explained as she led the way to the field behind the produce shed. "Start on the south side and work your way across. The boys ran the rototiller between the rows yesterday, so you'll just need to pull the weeds that are close to the plants. I'll be back in a couple of hours."

"What do I do with the weeds?" he asked.

A sharp retort sprang to mind, but she bit it back. "Throw them on the ground between the rows" was all she said before she walked away. Halfway back to the shed, she glanced back. He was staring across the two-acre field with an unreadable expression. Then he bent at the waist, pulled, and flung the weed aside.

Beth turned away. That should give him a taste of old-fashioned hard work, she thought as she hurried back to the truck. Then she remembered his soft palms, and in a fit of guilt, sent Robby out to the field with a pair of gloves. As she waited for him to return, she realized this arrangement might not work out as badly as she'd expected. Justin had already won over the teenagers and had proved himself capable enough. So why did she feel so uncomfortable around him? He was as arrogant as he was attractive, but she'd handled handsome, arrogant men before. It must be the consulting contract. Money altered everything, she'd found.

It was close to three hours later when the truck pulled back onto the Thompson Farm driveway. But Beth was jubilant with the afternoon's results. The restaurant's manager had been delighted with Beth's goods and had signed a three-month contract for produce.

After helping Robby unload the empty boxes, she sent him to the greenhouse to plant several flats of seedlings. As she headed to the house to check the answering machine, she noticed that Justin's suitcases were still in the back of the Jeep. Inside, the only sign that he'd been there was a dirty glass on the counter and a peanut-butter smeared knife. Thinking he'd had the right idea, she made a peanut-butter sandwich for herself. Then she saw the sheaf of papers tacked to the front of the refrigerator beneath several plastic flower magnets.

The contract. Justin must have put it there while she was gone. Well, she'd deal with that later. She figured chances were fifty-fifty that Justin hadn't found farming nearly as interesting as he'd anticipated. He might be ready to head back to California. Then she'd find herself in the dubious position of persuading him to stay—she needed the money that badly. With that in mind, she headed for the field to see how Justin had fared.

The afternoon temperature had climbed steadily, so she shouldn't have been surprised to find Justin's sweat-damp shirt slung over the gatepost. Peering out across the rows, she spotted him halfway across the field, bending and stretching, flinging handfuls of green into the pathways. His pale skin was already tinged with a hint of red.

Then he stood straight, arching his back and stretching, his arms held high above his head. As the sweat-glazed muscles rippled and burled in his shoulders, Beth decided she'd definitely misjudged him. The man was no layabout. Those were health-club muscles, she'd bet. No matter where he'd earned them, though, she knew he'd adapt to farm life better than someone who wasn't used to regular exercise. Maybe the next twelve weeks wouldn't be as bad as she thought.

Who was she kidding? It would be pure torment if she couldn't make herself ignore the man. Unless . . . unless she followed her instincts. But if she gave this attraction full rein, what then? Wouldn't the torment be that much worse at the end of the summer?

Justin saw her then and called out. She shook off her musings and forced a smile to her lips.

"Looks like you've been busy," she answered, and made her way between the parallel rows of broccoli to where he stood.

"I fixed myself some lunch. I hope you don't mind, but I was starving and there wasn't anyone else around."

Beth nodded. "The other two boys are working in the corn today. They probably didn't even know you're here. You've done a good job," she added, pointing toward the area he'd already weeded. Then she faltered when she noticed the wide, blank space between the cabbage and broccoli.

"What happened to the kale?"

"What's that?"

"Oh, no!" She reached that part of the field at a half-run. It was gone, an entire row of kale. Well, not exactly gone. The gray-green leafy plants lay in wilting piles between the rows. And her brand-new contract called for plenty of that particular vegetable.

Justin reached the empty space right on her heels. "I pulled something I shouldn't have." It wasn't a question. His apologetic tone softened the blow, but it didn't solve the sudden kale-supply problem.

Beth lifted one of the plants. "This isn't a weed." She explained what kale was and how popular it was with the chefs at several of the restaurants she supplied.

"Couldn't I replant them?" he suggested. "I pulled most of them out whole."

"Are you kidding? I think it's too late," she replied, shaking the wilting plant for emphasis and spraying herself with dirt in the process. She sputtered on the dirt, spit it off her tongue, and continued. "Look, I guess I should have explained better, but I was in a hurry. I figured you couldn't do too much damage here. My mistake."

Justin pulled off his gloves and flung them to the ground. "As you say, it's as much your fault as it is mine. How was I supposed to know?"

"You could have asked."

"Who?"

Beth glared. He was right, damn it. She spun and walked away. "Come on," she called. "I'll give you the tour, and we'll make sure nothing like this happens again. If you decide to stay, that is.''

"Wait a minute," Justin bellowed, grabbing her arm and whirling her around to face him. "What's that supposed to mean?"

Beth started to speak, then felt the heat radiating from his body, warmer than the sun at her back. And something fluttered beneath her ribs, capturing her breath. "I . . ." she began, but couldn't seem to concentrate on what she should say. Her eyes focused on the throbbing pulse at his throat, and a matching rhythm thudded in her ears.

"Do you want me to leave?" he asked.

"No." She pulled away from him, away from his disturbing touch. "I just meant that you might not want to stay here, not after seeing what farm life's really all about. It's hard work. It's hot or it's cold, but seldom in between. And it can be pretty boring to someone who's used to more sophisticated entertainment."

"Do you find it boring?"

Beth smiled. "Never."

"Then I don't guess I'll be bored. Tired, maybe," he said, rubbing the small of his back. "But not bored."

Beth angled her head, eyeing him thoughtfully. "You're sure you want to go through with this? Because if you do, you'll have to carry your share of the load. Today wasn't an exception. We work like this every day. And I'm not going to make it easy on you, not if you still want to get the feel of farming."

Justin met her gaze in a head-on challenge. "I can take anything you dish out," he replied silkily. "Anything."

"Good," she replied. "Follow me. And put your shirt on. You're starting to burn."

FIVE

The sun had sunk low on the horizon when the combined effects of rampaging mosquitoes and gnawing hunger drove them indoors. As they entered the house, an aged, warbling soprano belted out a rousing rendition of "Amazing Grace."

"Aunt Eva!" Beth cried, and hurried toward the kitchen with a newfound lift to her step. Justin grimaced and limped along behind, feeling the fatigue in every muscle of his body. Today he'd used muscles he'd forgotten he had, muscles he suspected hadn't been stretched and strained since college when he'd worked summers repairing water mains and filling potholes.

When he reached the doorway, he noticed a pair of floury handprints on the back of Beth's shirt. "You could have stayed in town," she was saying. "We could manage for a few days more."

The older woman belatedly wiped her hands on her apron. "Couldn't have the two of you sleepin' in this house alone. Reverend Thomas agreed and was kind enough to give me a ride home. Couldn't talk him into staying for supper, though."

"Oh, for Pete's sake," Beth muttered.

"Besides," the woman continued, as if her great-niece hadn't even spoken. "Nobody should be subjected to your cookin' for two meals straight. Oh, and I almost forgot. I picked up those books you asked me to look for. They're on your dresser."

"Thanks, Aunt Eva," Beth said with a wary look toward Justin.

"Anything I can do to help. I'm glad you decided to—"

"When will supper be ready, Aunt Eva?" Beth interrupted.

"A few minutes," the older woman responded with a puzzled frown. She lifted a floured pork chop and slid it gently into a skillet full of grease. Watching it sizzle and pop, Justin felt the beginnings of a full-fledged rumble in his stomach.

"Nice to see you again, ma'am," he said, rubbing the threatening portion of his anatomy. "I'll just go wash up and change for dinner."

Aunt Eva shook the spatula at him. "Stop right there, young man," she ordered. "No need to fancy up. Save that for Sunday."

Justin backed up another step and sucked his stomach in further, hoping to control the rumbling. "I got a bit sweaty working in the sun today," he explained. "I'd better clean up."

"You can't smell any worse than Charley," Aunt Eva said. "Beth? He doesn't, does he?"

"I—umm—" Beth stuttered, and a slow flush crept up her neck and flooded her face. "I hadn't noticed." Intrigued, Justin studied her expression. He was disappointed when she averted her eyes, but even that gesture was telling. And while his mind was distracted,

his protesting stomach reacted full force to the tantalizing odor of cooking food, rumbling out of control over
the sound of the sizzling meat.

Aunt Eva chuckled. "Get washed up so you can feed
that thing, boy. Can't live on peanut butter."

"Hurry," Beth whispered as they left the kitchen.
"Before the pork chops get hard. She won't take them
out of the pan until we're seated at the table."

Justin's eyes widened. "Why?"

"They might get cold," she said, then pointed down
the hall. "You take that one, and I'll use the bathroom
upstairs. Last one done gets blamed for the food."

Justin was quicker, but not by much. He'd just
reached the staircase when he heard Beth's step near
the top.

"Phew, that feels better," Justin admitted as he
stopped to wait for her. "I was beginning to itch."

Beth didn't answer until she reached the bottom step.
"It's probably the tomatoes you brushed against.
Unless you picked up a couple of insects." Her eyes
met his, then drifted sideways, focusing somewhere
near his left ear.

"No," he said. "I'm not falling for that one."

"Really," she insisted. "There's something there."

He felt the faint brush of her fingers against his
cheek, then in his hair. She waved a yellowed leaf
before his eyes, then held it up to the light.

"Apple, I think. What were you doing in the
orchard?"

"Hunting for lunch."

She looked alarmed. "You didn't eat anything, did
you? Green apples, when you're not used to them, will
give you . . . well, they can cause problems."

He knew what she meant. "There were green apples

where I grew up," he pointed out, enjoying her discomfiture. She'd assumed so much about him, most of it wrong. He was going to enjoy surprising her with the truth.

She nodded, reaching for the ring. She turned it over in her fingers, rubbing at the dirt that marred the silver vein that threaded through the polished turquoise stone. "I've never seen anything like this," she said.

"A friend of mine, a jewelry designer, gave it to me. I bought the stone from a Zuni Indian when I was filming in Arizona a few years ago."

Beth nodded. "You'd better leave it in the house tomorrow. You'll ruin it otherwise." She pointed toward the door. "The pork chops," she reminded him.

Dinner was quiet but pleasant at the old oak table in the kitchen. The broccoli was overcooked to almost an olive-green, but the pork chop was fairly tender, thanks to the quick wash-up. He shuddered to think what he might have been forced to eat if he'd taken time for a shower.

"How is Charley?" he asked when Aunt Eva got up to fetch the strawberry pie.

"He threw his crutches at one of the nurses today. He doesn't have a walking cast yet," she explained for Justin's benefit. "The doctor says it'll be a few more weeks, after the knee's recovered more from the surgery. Something about the ligaments healing right."

Justin frowned. "Sounds serious. And painful."

"It wouldn't be if he'd take the pills," Aunt Eva muttered. "Stubborn old coot."

"Did the doctor say when he can come home?"

"End of the week. Maybe," she said. "But he'll have more surgery on that knee later."

Glancing up from his plate, Justin caught the worried

look that passed between the two women. "You know," he said. "My grandfather was older than Charley when he had knee surgery. Joint replacement or something like that. He's still getting around just fine."

The forced smiles of the two women indicated they appreciated his gesture, but he hadn't accomplished much in the way of reassuring them. Not knowing what else to say, he excused himself and fetched his suitcases from the Jeep. An hour later, after taking a quick shower and unpacking, he slipped back downstairs to see what Beth had in store for him the next day.

He paused on the stair landing and ran his fingers over the darkened, smooth railing. Oak, he'd bet, and wondered how it would look stripped and refinished. The threadbare stair runner spoke of years and generations of footfalls, and he could sense the souls that had once filled the place. Some old houses were like that, he mused. They oozed with atmosphere and memories. Beth's house was solid, built to house generations of children. It needed a lot of work, granted, but houses like this were as irreplaceable as memories.

He was tempted to slide across the polished wood floor, but the thought of misjudging and crashing into the china cabinet halted the impulse. Following the sound of voices, he returned to the kitchen, pausing in the doorway.

The two women were huddled over the contract he'd brought, both frowning.

"Wait a minute," Beth said. "Read this part to me. It's not making any sense."

As the older woman read, comprehension dawned across Beth's face and she relaxed. "That's fine. Now what about the next part?"

Aunt Eva nodded and muttered something. She

pointed and read again. The pattern continued for another five minutes before Justin slipped away. Upstairs in his room, he pondered the strange tableaux he'd just witnessed. It reminded him of years past when he and Mel had struggled to make sense of algebra and English literature, with the somewhat dubious help of their parents. But why would Beth have trouble understanding the contract? The terms were simple and straightforward, without a trace of legalese. It was as if she couldn't read.

No. That was ridiculous. Of course she could read. She was a bright, intelligent woman. He thought about the evening they'd spent in Kansas City and remembered how she'd frowned over the press release and crib sheets Melanie had prepared. No, she was just suspicious of him, probably searching for hidden clauses or implications. Why shouldn't she? A lot of money was involved.

Quietly retreating to his room, he read in bed until long after he heard the two women come upstairs. Justin wasn't sure when he drifted off to sleep. But when he awoke the next morning, he'd have pledged his firstborn child for ten minutes in his jacuzzi. The simple act of sitting up was an agony. Walking was worse.

His usual morning run was out of the question, but ten minutes of stretching exercises eased the pain. Slowly, he gathered up a change of clothes and eased his way across the room to the door.

A folded sheaf of papers lay just inside the room, one corner still tucked under the six-panel door. His muscles protested as he bent to retrieve it, but he simply gritted his teeth and grabbed the papers. There was no note, no explanation, only Beth's scrawled signature on the last page. And that was explanation enough. He was here to stay, for twelve weeks at least.

The next three days were worse than he'd expected. Beth seemed determined to break him with one onerous task after another. No sooner had he finished weeding the onions than she handed him a pitchfork and shovel for mucking out the barn. He was still ankle-deep in manure when she discovered a gaping hole in the roof of the tumbledown hayshed. Since there was nothing much left to nail a patch to, the hay had to be moved, every last bale, to a dry spot in the big barn loft.

Justin fell into bed each night after supper, sinking almost immediately into an exhausted sleep despite his blisters and aches. He awoke each morning a little less stiff and sore and a lot happier than he'd been in a long time. He attributed this odd bliss to the lack of city stresses. Or maybe it was the dual challenge of the unaccustomed physical labor and the wall of reserve Beth had built between them.

Then Charley came home, growling, grumping, and railing against his infirmity and the new diet the doctor had imposed. Charley filled the hours between supper and bedtime with a litany of complaints, broken only by the clacking of Aunt Eva's knitting needles and the rustle of papers from Beth's office.

Beth seemed oblivious to it, working there behind the closed door, and Justin began to wonder what she did in there that was so time-consuming. She only came out was during the weather report, and that didn't do much to improve her mood since the forecaster couldn't promise the much-needed rain would appear.

Justin had thought that if they could relax together when the work was finished, they'd get to know each other. They could pick up where they'd left off in the

Jaguar, before she'd gotten angry with him. Apparently, Beth preferred otherwise. Or maybe this place made it impossible for her to relax these days.

It was in the midst of one of those complaining sessions that Beth's patience snapped.

"Enough," Beth shouted. Justin looked up from the sports section, startled to see her stamping through the room until she stood directly in front of the old man's tattered, overstuffed chair. She'd exchanged her work clothes for a shirtwaist dress and heels. He found himself paying more attention to the curve of her calves than the din she was creating. She must have changed while he was out for a walk. But why? Was she expecting someone? The thought made him uneasy.

"Go ahead," Beth was taunting as she snatched a bag of pork rinds from Charley's fingers. "Eat all that junk and clog up your arteries again. And while you're at it, why don't you take a stroll around the farm and see if you can rip all the stitches out of your knee and maybe tear a ligament or two. Or just keep complaining and maybe we'll all help you to an early grave."

Charley's jaw dropped, then his eyes narrowed and he sniffed theatrically. "What's that smell?" He winked over at Justin. "Smells like some sort of flower."

"Are you even listening to me?"

Charley leaned back and lifted the paper. "I guess that young vet's coming courtin' again. That or you broke a bottle of perfume."

Beth faltered, then sniffed. "Too much?" she asked.

Aunt Eva thumped her knitting down. "That's enough, you old goat. I've got some chair seats that need caning. I'll go get the stuff."

"I'll help," Justin said, ready to escape.

Behind him, Charley snorted. "Don't know how to do that. Take 'em to town."

Beth grabbed a book off the shelf and threw it in his lap. "Look it up. And stop complaining so much."

Justin let the door slam shut behind him and followed Aunt Eva to the detached garage behind the house. "Don't pay him any mind," the old woman said. "He's just bored and tired of being cooped up."

"We'll just have to think of something to keep him busy," he replied. "I've noticed a few screens that need mending. And couldn't he take over some of the bookwork? Beth spends too much time cooped up in that office."

The older woman turned away, an odd expression on her face. "You'd better talk to Beth."

Five minutes later, Justin maneuvered the last of the broken chairs through the front door. A loud squawk sounded next to his ear as Edgar swooped through the opening and landed on the newel post. Then he flapped his glossy black wings, circling the room before disappearing into the upper hallway.

"Drat, the jewelry box is open," Beth muttered, heading for the stairs. When Justin started to follow, she protested. "I'll chase him back down and you try and shoo him out the door."

There ensued a series of muffled thumps and bangs, punctuated with a few clearly enunciated curses which trailed downstairs, making Charley chuckle. Then the bird sailed down the open stairwell and landed on the lampshade beside Charley's chair. The shiny metal dangling from his beak glittered and flashed in the lamplight.

"My ring," Justin exclaimed, lunging for the bird. Startled, Edgar took flight, emitting a throaty squawk without once opening his beak and dropping the ring. He circled the room twice, then settled on the vintage chandelier that hung in the entryway.

"Careful. Don't scare him or he'll fly off again," Beth warned as Justin gingerly climbed onto one of the damaged chairs, carefully balancing his feet on the wooden frame to avoid the tattered cane seat. The chair wobbled and shifted and Beth grabbed the back of it.

"Hold it steady," Justin said. "I don't care if he flies off. Just so he drops the ring. It's handmade. One of a kind."

"It would be," Beth muttered, shifting and bracing her foot on the chair run. Her cheek brushed against his leg, then she reached around to hold each side of the seat. Her firm, warm breast touched his calf, retreated, then touched again.

Justin sent her what he hoped was a quelling look, but she didn't seem the least bit intimidated. Perhaps she hadn't noticed. *How could she not notice?* His flesh burned, and he feared his body would soon betray the surge of lust that had flooded him at the light touch.

"Pull his tail feathers," Charley suggested as Justin reached toward the bird.

"Not over the rug," Aunt Eva warned. "He'll mess on it."

A light knock sounded at the door, then the screen swung open.

"Need any help?" a smooth, deep voice asked. The lean, blond man stood poised in the open doorway. With his neatly combed hair and dressed in a freshly ironed shirt and pleated twill pants, he looked ready for church. Or a date, Justin added mentally, noting the faint odor of cologne.

"Shut the door," Justin ordered.

"What?"

Relllk! Squawk! With a flutter of black, Edgar swooped through the open space and out into the evening air.

"Damn!" Justin shouted and glared down at the visitor. The lean blond man gaped back, perplexed.

"What's going on?" he asked.

"Sorry, Ross," Beth answered as she helped Justin down from the chair. "Edgar's up to his old tricks. He got Justin's ring this time, a valuable one."

When Ross looked expectantly at Justin. "You must be the new hired hand," Ross said. "You know, the guys were right. You bear an amazing resemblance to the guy on *Vice Cops*, what's his name? Justin something?"

Justin held out his hand, masking his irritation. "Odd, isn't it? I keep hearing that, but I just don't see the resemblance, especially with the beard and all."

Ross grinned as they shook hands. "Something about your eyes, I guess. Probably the name doesn't help, either."

"Carl Justin Schnell, really," Justin explained. "So you're the local veterinarian. I guess Beth and the others keep you pretty busy." He released Ross's hand and waited, fixing a challenging stare on him.

"Busy enough."

"Guess that doesn't leave much time for a social life," Justin commented.

Beth cleared her throat and cast a warning glance at Justin. Why, he couldn't fathom. It wasn't as if he was threatening the guy or even being rude.

"I'll just be a minute. I left my purse in the other room," she said. She dashed into the kitchen and back again so quickly that Justin got the distinct impression she was afraid to leave the two men alone. "Let's get going," she suggested, practically shoving the man out the door and glaring when Justin followed them onto the porch.

She glanced back once on the way to the pickup truck, and Justin blew her a kiss. Her mouth fell open in shock, then clamped shut as she turned away.

"Where's he taking her?" he asked Aunt Eva after the couple had left.

"An ice cream social at the church. The Sunday school classes are supposed to put on skits, I believe."

"Hmm," he rubbed his whiskers thoughtfully.

"Ross is a widower. Lost his wife a few years ago in a farm accident."

What a date, he mused. The ice cream social in a pickup truck with the widower veterinarian. It seemed so old-fashioned, so small-townish. So normal. "I'd have taken her if I knew she wanted to go," he said aloud.

"The girl hasn't been to one of those things since her grandmother died," Aunt Eva replied as she picked up her knitting. "If you ask me, she's been acting strange lately. Must be something to do with the weather—not a drop of rain since you came."

Justin grinned. Somehow he didn't think Beth's odd behavior had anything to do with the weather.

The moon was high in the sky when Ross's pickup truck pulled into the gravel parking area behind the peeling old house.

"I'm thirsty, how about you? Aunt Eva probably left some tea in the refrigerator," Beth said as she climbed out of the cab.

"Sounds good," Ross answered, following her up

the walk to the porch. While he settled into one of the wicker chairs, Beth let herself in the house. Charley's snore rumbled through the door of the downstairs bedroom, but aside from that, the house was silent. Someone had left a light on in the living room, so she turned it off, then made tall, iced teas for the two of them. They spent a pleasant twenty minutes or so just talking. Then they lapsed into a companionable silence.

"What made you change your mind?" Ross finally said. "I've been asking you out for two years, and you've been politely refusing."

Beth shrugged. "I've been working pretty hard lately, ever since Charley was hurt. I just needed to get out."

"That's all?" He sounded disappointed, and a stirring of guilt prompted her to lay her hand on his.

"That and your wonderful company," she quipped. "Not to mention the glorious entertainment." The skits performed by the Sunday school classes had been the same time-worn skits she'd performed at that age. Only the mishaps and improvisations of the youngsters changed.

"Well, it's late and I'd best be going," he said, rising and pulling Beth with him to the porch steps. Standing one step down, they were at eye level, and Beth didn't draw away when he leaned closer.

His kiss was gentle and undemanding without a hint of passion. Nothing stirred beneath her ribs, and her knees held firm and strong.

" 'Night," Ross murmured. "See you in church."

She watched the truck back away, turn, and point down the drive. She followed its movement until the taillights disappeared from sight around the corner. Then she noticed a ladder positioned under the old mulberry tree at the edge of the drive. What was it doing there? Surely Aunt Eva hadn't taken a mind to make mulberry cobbler, not with the berries from that tree. They were as bland as hospital soup, maybe worse.

Just then, something brown dropped from the tree with a thump. Then a foot descended from the branches and rested on the top step.

"Instead of standing there with that lovesick expression, you could hold this darn ladder," Justin growled.

The stirring she'd missed before danced beneath her ribs. Justin! But what was he doing in the tree? Besides watching her and Ross.

Her hands bunched into fists at her hips and she snorted. "Get down yourself. That's what you get for spying like an adolescent little brother."

"Unless you want to spend the night filling out insurance papers at the emergency room, you'd better get over here and hold this miserable excuse for a ladder," he barked back.

Beth hesitated, then considered the very real possibility of Justin falling. She kicked off the spike-heeled shoes and turned her back, then popped the stockings loose from the garters. Stockings did have certain advantages over panty hose. This time, at least, they'd been convenient instead of a further source of embarrassment.

"What are you doing?" he demanded.

"Stockings cost money. I don't want them full of runs."

"You didn't wear that pink garter for him, did you?"

Beth dropped the skirt and whirled around. "What pink garter?"

"The one you wore at the Hyatt," he reminded her.

Beth's face flamed, and she was grateful for the darkness under the trees. "None of your business," she

*What would I have done if he hadn't stopped? Would
we have made love there on the porch?* But in the next
breath, she chastised herself for an overactive imagination. It was just a kiss, after all. *Or was it?*

The questions wouldn't go away and stop torturing
her. Twice Sunday afternoon and once during church,
she caught herself staring off into the distance, day-
dreaming. She'd hidden behind the shed and watched
Justin carry grain to the cattle. She studied him from
behind a newspaper while he let Charley win at bot-
tlecap poker in the evening. Even when she closeted
herself in the office to study, she couldn't concentrate
for listening to the low hum of voices and the occasional vibrant rumble of laughter.

She had to stop this! It was madness, she told herself
early Monday morning as she turned down the short
path to the greenhouse. If she kept up this way, she
wouldn't pass the high school equivalency test, and she
still wouldn't have a diploma. The man was interfering
too much in her life.

She forced her thoughts away from him and tried to

concentrate on the day ahead. Her wrist was still sore and slightly swollen. Wrapped as it was with an elastic bandage, she thought she'd be able to handle her work if she was careful. With that in mind, she decided to let Justin and Robby handle the deliveries. Better that than sending Robby alone and spending another day like yesterday, watching for Justin from around every corner.

In the distance, she heard Justin whistling and she hurriedly slipped into the damp, earthy-smelling green-house. During the summer months, with the outdoor gardens in full production, they used the greenhouse only for storage. Lately, though, they'd done little more than throw the empty crates and boxes through the door. The result was a jumbled mess that blocked the narrow passages between the growing benches. Frowning, Beth began stacking and organizing with a frenzy.

Within half an hour she'd restored a semblance of order, and she stopped to stretch. As she glanced up, she saw him watching from the other side of the glass. His brooding gaze warmed Beth in a way she couldn't comprehend. It wasn't simply the desire that shimmered in his darkening blue eyes and in the tense, aching set of his mouth. Something deeper and infinitely more stirring radiated between them, something so strong it was almost tangible.

The tremor that started in her fingertips and spread to her limbs, even to her lips, was real, though, and she instinctively leaned back against a bench. When Justin followed the glass wall to the door, she didn't move. His eyes never left hers and she was struck with an eerie sense of unreality, like she was watching a movie, a scripted suspense designed to keep the audience at the edge of its collective seat.

Forcing herself to break eye contact, she glanced down at the very real goose bumps on her arm and reached for a crate, moving it needlessly from one pile to the other. The door squeaked open, but she refused to look up. She didn't dare, for fear her emotions were written across her face. She didn't want him to see what she was feeling then—the confusion, the swelling surge of desire that made even her toes tingle.

"Beth?"

She plunked the box down and moved another. "Is Robby here yet?"

"He called a few minutes ago. He's not coming."

Beth turned, the damp stack of boxes forgotten. "Robby's sick?" The boy hadn't missed work in the two years he'd been in her employ. He'd only been late once, and only then because of a flash flood that washed out a bridge.

Justin shrugged. "He didn't say. He wants you to call him right back." His message delivered, he pulled open the aluminum door, then hesitated. "About the other night . . ." he began, then faltered.

Beth reached for a box, then balanced it in front of her. "Moonlight and freshly mown grass can be a pretty powerful combination out here in the country if you let it go to your head."

The door clattered shut. "Don't kid yourself," Justin said in a husky tone.

Beth dislodged the lump in her throat so she could speak. But when she met his eyes, her voice nearly deserted her. "It was just a kiss," she finally said. It was much more than that to her, but she'd die before she'd let him know how she'd relived his kisses in her thoughts. His desire was obvious, but he'd desired many women and probably had been desired by more than she could imagine. What was one more?

He took a step toward her, and she pulled the box protectively against her chest. "It wasn't *just* anything. You enjoyed it as much as I did," he said.

She thrust the box against him and sidestepped out of his reach. "I think that we'd both better get to work since we're shorthanded today. Fill that with beets, and get a few from the experimental patch. I want to take some of the golden ones in for samples today."

"You're changing the subject."

"That's right," she said. "I'm your boss. That gives me the right to change the subject whenever I feel like it."

"You're chicken."

"Maybe," she answered, then gasped when he snagged her arm as she slid past. His grip was firm, but not hard enough to hurt. Just the opposite, in fact, as she noted the soft rub of the newly formed calluses against her skin.

"You feel it, too." he insisted, the blue of his eyes deepening with temper. "Don't tell me you don't because I know better." He touched the throbbing vein in her throat, then glanced pointedly at the hardening nipples showing through her thin bra and T-shirt.

"All right," she admitted. "I'm attracted to you. I just have no intention of acting like a fool about it. You're bored, and I happen to be the only woman around who's of an age to amuse you. If Aunt Eva were thirty years younger, you'd probably be sweet-talking her in the moonlight, too."

The finger trailed from the vein up to her chin, then back behind her ear to cup her face. "Take a chance," he said.

She shook her head and pulled his hand away. "I can't." She left him standing there as she hurried out of the greenhouse and up the path to the packing shed before she forgot what happened to foolish women who let their passions rule them. She slipped inside and leaned against the wall for a minute to collect herself.

Take a chance, he'd said. And she was right to say no. She couldn't live like Marlene. She had too much of her grandmother in her for that. No, when she let herself love a man, it would be someone who would stick around and not move on to brighter lights and false stars at summer's end.

With her emotions still running high, she reacted more out of fear than common sense when Robby called again to tell her he was quitting. He'd been offered a job on a construction crew at twice what Beth could afford to pay. She couldn't blame him for snapping up the job, but his lack of notice left her in the lurch, especially with Charley still laid up.

The immediate problem was that day's round of deliveries, a duty she'd shared with Robby since Charley's accident. She'd given the other boys, all cousins, the day off to attend a family reunion in Iowa. That left Justin.

"Bad news?" he said as he carried a basket of tomatoes through the door and over to the packing table.

Her scowl deepened, partly because the news *was* bad and partly because she wasn't ready to face him. "Robby quit." She explained about the construction job and how the boy was saving money to pay for his college tuition.

"We'll manage," Justin said. "I guess I could make the deliveries if you'll give me a list."

Beth drew a deep breath and considered. Charley had

always handled the route on his own, and so could she under normal circumstances. But with her wrist still tender, she couldn't manage the rough steering and stiff gear box of the delivery truck.

"What if someone recognizes you?" she asked.

He shrugged. "I've been to town a few times and no one's noticed. I guess it's the beard. Or maybe the TV reception is so fuzzy out here that they wouldn't recognize me without it, either."

Beth wasn't in the mood for weak jokes, though. "You'd have to stop at two restaurants in downtown Kansas City and one on the plaza. They get great reception there."

"I must have overestimated my popularity in this part of the country. Nobody recognized me a month ago. I doubt they'll recognize me now," he admitted. "You could go along to run interference this first time and to make sure I don't get lost."

Reluctantly, Beth agreed. It was the only solution that made sense. Besides, she was being ridiculous. What could happen while delivering vegetables in broad daylight?

She'd almost convinced herself by the time she climbed into the cab and buckled her seat belt. The truck started easily under Justin's coaxing hand. However, Beth's relieved smile faded as he ground the gears, missed reverse, and hit a fencepost. Somehow, though, he managed to get the truck rolling in the right direction without hitting anything else. At first, their progress was a series of rough, jolting lurches down the drive. She reached out to brace herself with her good hand.

"Try not to foul up what's left of the transmission," she said, ignoring Justin's irritated glare.

"How old is she?"

"Who?" Beth threw a puzzled glance his way before a jolting bump reminded her of the seat-belt buckle dangling from her fingertips.

"The truck." His exasperated tone indicated he thought she was being particularly obtuse.

"It's a '65," she answered. "Grandma bought it from Mr. Sayles at the lumberyard in '75 or '76."

He chuckled. "She. Not it."

"Oh, Lord. You aren't one of those guys who names his car and whispers sweet nothings to it."

"No. I save my sweet nothings for more rewarding subjects," he taunted, then shifted again, wincing when the gears clicked and groaned.

"Maybe you'd better try a few now. Or maybe I should have driven after all."

"Yeah, and you could seriously damage that wrist."

"It beats dying."

He stared over and quirked a doubting eyebrow before glancing back at the road. "Has this gear box always been this stiff?"

Beth shrugged. "I suppose. Sure you don't want to trade places?"

"I'll get the hang of it," he insisted. True to his word, his next gear change barely jarred the cab, and there was only the tiniest clunk from the transmission.

"Better?" he prompted.

"I guess you can save your sweet nothings," she replied.

"Something tells me it'll take more than sweet nothings to get what I want."

"And that is?"

He stared straight ahead. For a moment she thought he wasn't going to answer. Perhaps he hadn't heard her. She'd already turned her eyes to the blurred land-scape outside her window when the single syllable he uttered jarred her more soundly than any stalling lurch the truck was capable of.

"You," she thought he said. No, she'd misunder-stood. Her imagination was affecting her hearing. Her startled eyes studied his profile, but his expression told her nothing. Until he looked at her. The smoldering promise in his eyes sent shivers up her spine—warm, delicious shivers that seemed at odds with the heat in the cab. She rolled down the window, but the whipping wind didn't cool her.

"You turn left at the next intersection," she said, changing the subject.

Beth waited in the truck on their first stop, another produce farm that would supply the kale to fill most of her orders. After that, she handled the invoices and collected the checks while Justin unloaded the truck. But it didn't matter that she kept her distance, that if she talked at all, it was only to tell him where to turn, where to park, or what to take out of the truck. Her body was throbbingly aware of his nearness.

She'd just come out of the tiny office of a restaurant halfway through the route when the manager called her back.

"Roberto is working on a new side dish," the portly man said as he reared back in his chair. "He wants some of those yellow beets, the ones that don't bleed. We'll see how this experiment of his turns out. If it's good, we'll talk again."

Beth headed for the truck, momentarily distracted by the prospect of new orders. She climbed into the back and rummaged around for the beets. Finding them, she chose a few, then twisted in the narrow aisle between the stacked crates to deposit them in a box. As she turned, she caught sight of a body blocking the exit and her heart leaped into her throat at Justin's sudden appearance.

"Did I startle you?" Justin asked.

"I didn't hear you," she answered in a breathy voice. "Must be all the traffic noise. I can barely hear myself think."

Justin shrugged. "They say you get used to it, but I never did." Beth stared thoughtfully at his back as he lifted a crate, then started toward the open door.

"Justin?" Her voice was low, but he turned halfway around.

"Yeah?"

"Do you ever wonder what your life would be like if you weren't an actor? If you hadn't made all that money?"

She half expected a glib retort, but he stared pensively into the crate as if the cabbages could bestow great wisdom. When he finally looked up, his eyes were troubled and vulnerable. "I try not to think about it," he answered, then slowly eased himself out of the truck and carried the box through the restaurant's back door. Puzzled by his answer, Beth absently picked up the box and followed. Chef Roberto met her just inside the door.

"You have the beets?"

She forced herself to smile up at the man in the white apron and held out the box. "Right here," she said, then stepped aside as Justin passed on his way back to the truck for another load.

Roberto's broad grin faded as he reached into the box. Thoughts of Justin faded into the background as she watched the man's expression change from delight to puzzlement to disgust. Good heavens, she'd missed a bug! Then she noticed the box itself. It wasn't the one she'd packed the beets into. It wasn't even the same size.

Shaking his head, the chef reached in and picked up a long white icicle radish, then a bright red one. "This is a beet?"

Beth sighed and took the radishes from him. "I picked up the wrong box," she said, backing away. She half ran out to the truck and leaped inside, bumping hard into Justin as he negotiated the narrow aisle with another large crate.

The radishes flew in several directions as Beth fell backward. The box Justin was carrying landed on top of her. He stumbled, recovered, then slipped on a rolling radish to land with a thump on top of his box, knocking most of the breath out of her.

Beth grunted and shoved against the weight pressing her down. "Get up," she croaked. "Get it off me."

Justin started to rise, but his shoe clipped her thigh and she yelped. "Sorry," he muttered. "But there's not a whole lot of room to maneuver here." Finally, he managed to lever himself off of the box and lift it.

"Phew!" Beth wheezed. "What's in there?"

"More cabbage. Are you hurt?"

"I'll live." She lay there for an instant as her breathing eased, not daring to move yet, not while his left foot touched her ear and the other pressed close to her side. Lean, denim-clad legs stretched above her, straddling her as he set the cabbages aside.

"Help me up," she demanded. "This bed of radishes is lumpy."

A flaring heat in his expression told her he'd like to

see her on a very different sort of bed, and she felt herself blush.

"Give me your hand. I won't bite it," he said when she hesitated. "Isn't there some cliché about biting the hand that signs your paycheck?"

Beth grimaced, but she raised her arm high, grasped his outstretched hand, and let him pull her to her feet. Instead of releasing her, he pulled her close, holding her sore wrist carefully, then unrolling the elastic bandage.

"Are you all right? You didn't twist this again, did you? Or anything else?" His concern touched her, softening her resistance. He seemed genuinely upset.

"I'm fine."

"You're sure? You're not just saying that like before?"

"A few bumps, but no real harm," she insisted and reached up to smooth away the worried frown. The touch was his undoing, and the last remnants of control fell away, revealing the banked fires that smoldered behind his darkening eyes.

"I'm going to kiss you again," he warned.

"Just this once," she whispered, pressing closer, her lips a hairsbreadth from his. Then she closed the distance, or maybe he did. It didn't matter who touched first, for the sun beating on the roof of the truck was nothing to the heat between them as skin touched skin.

It lasted mere seconds, but the sweetness of it held as they drew apart.

"Someday, Beth Ann Thompson," he said. "Someday I won't have to trick you or fall on you to kiss you."

Her lips curved, but her voice was serious as she shook her head. "I don't think so."

"I care about you."

She backed away, shaking her head. "In a few weeks you'll be gone. I can't love that lightly."

"It could be fantastic."

"Or a disaster," she replied, and reached for the box of beets, finding the right one this time. "I don't play in your league. In fact, I don't play at all." She headed out into the bright sunlight.

"You're lying," he called after her. "You're playing right now."

She considered for a moment. "Maybe for a moment I thought about it, following your lead and letting these feelings play themselves out. But I can't do it. It's not in me to be so casual about sex."

"I don't recall asking you to go to bed with me yet."

She looked up without a trace of the sad smile she'd had for him a moment ago. "Let's keep it that way," she retorted, before turning her back and stalking into the restaurant, the box clutched tightly against her breasts.

He stared after her, perplexed. She felt it, too, he knew, this tugging, tearing sensation that left him hard and wanting whenever she was near enough to touch. The green flecks in her eyes darkened at the merest brush of his fingertips, sometimes without even a touch.

But she seemed determined to keep her distance. Even when they kissed, she held something back, some part of herself that she couldn't seem to put at risk. *Don't we all?* he asked himself, and wondered whether she sensed the shadowed memories that allowed him to pursue, but only so far. Into bed, but never into intimacy. He never shared his private thoughts, his private dreams, even the very private, very expensive home he'd made within hearing of the low breakers that beat against the bay shore.

"You're afraid," he told her when she joined him a few minutes later in the truck cab. His hand brushed her cheek and she unconsciously leaned into his touch.

"Maybe I am. I have my reasons."

"Who hurt you?"

She met his eyes and gave her head a slight shake. Her reasons were too complicated to explain to him. He hadn't lived her life, hadn't watched Marlene's struggles to survive on her own. How could she tell him that once she allowed herself to need someone, she might not be able to cope alone again? "It doesn't matter" was all she said.

"We'll go slow," Justin said.

_____ SEVEN _____

A cloud of dust hovered over the road as Justin guided the old truck from the highway onto the Thompson Farm driveway, and they quickly rolled up the windows. The airless heat was better than choking on dust, though not by much.

"Looks like you've got company," Justin said. "Expecting anyone? Your mother, maybe?"

"She's still in Europe. Rome, I think," Beth muttered. "Damn, I knew we were running late. What time is it?"

Justin glanced sharply at Beth before checking his watch. "Quarter to twelve."

Beth's frown eased. "We're not that late. I guess Ross is early."

"You have a date?" His face was a study of nonchalance, but his hand tightened on the shift, and he released the clutch too quickly, jolting the truck.

"We have an appointment," she replied when the gears stopped protesting.

"Oh" was his only answer.

Beth took a deep breath. She didn't want anything

to destroy the delicate emotions they'd aroused that morning, even though she still had plenty of doubts. Justin showed distinct signs of jealousy, and she didn't know whether to be thrilled or worried.

"Ross is taking me over to a place near St. Joseph to look over some Angus calves," she explained. "The demand for organically raised beef is skyrocketing."

Justin's eyebrows raised thoughtfully. "I always figured it was a gimmick to jack the price up."

"Nope. It's the same principle as organic vegetables. Safe for the body, safe for the environment."

"Ahh. No chemical-nuked grain in the feedbox."

"Yeah. No growth stimulants. No antibiotics in the feed. That sort of thing."

"What about milk?" Justin suggested as the truck chugged through the dust up the hill. He stretched taller in the seat, probably scanning the farm for Ross's truck.

Beth shook her head as she answered. "Too much of an investment in cows and equipment, not to mention the cost of renovating the barn to accommodate it all and comply with health regulations."

"So why do you need Ross? You know what to look for, don't you? You and I could go."

He was jealous. Beth sighed, feeling a big uneasy about an encounter between the two men just now. "Ross is going to check on a brucellosis outbreak out that way and offered to take me along. These calves are at a nearby farm. I'd like him to look at them before I buy them."

"Sorry," he said. "I didn't mean to push. I guess it really isn't my business. Yet." The emphasis he placed on that final word warmed her. One word, filled with promise and possibilities. If she didn't guard her heart better, she'd start believing in those possibilities.

Maybe she already did, but she wasn't ready to be that honest, not even with herself.

They both spotted the distinctly marked Federal Express van at the same time. "Looks like the vet isn't here yet after all," Justin said, relaxing. He grasped her hand and pulled it to his lips for a quick kiss before he downshifted and eased the truck into the space next to the shed. As he turned off the engine, the Federal Express van speeded back down the driveway.

It took only a few minutes to unload the truck, since they'd already dropped the extra produce at a soup kitchen. Then they headed to the house for lunch and to see what the Federal Express man had left.

Charley tossed the fat, padded envelope at Justin as he came through the door. "Is that all the fan mail you get, boy?" the old man chortled. "I'da thought you'd do better than that."

Justin raised an eyebrow, thinking of the huge bags that arrived at the studio daily for the "Vice Cops" cast. "Guess I need to change my image," he said as he ripped open the package from his agent. He pulled the revised script out with a satisfied grunt. That would give him something to do in the evenings besides listen for Beth's movements in the office.

"That's a heck of a letter," Charley prompted.

Noting the blatant curiosity on the old man's face, Justin grinned. "My agent sent the script. He thinks I should start learning my lines." He flipped through the first few pages, paused, and grunted before heading for the stairs, his head bent in preoccupation.

"I guess this means you'll be too busy for a game of poker after dinner," Charley called after him.

Justin halted, balancing a hand on the newel post. "Old man, if you think I'm going to let you keep all my Coke caps, you're sadly mistaken. Your luck's bound to run out sooner or later.''

"It ain't luck, boy, and you know it," Charley retorted, winking over at Beth as he spoke. "For somebody who's supposed to be an actor, you're mighty poor at bluffin'.''

"How do you know I haven't been letting you win?"

Taken aback, Charley straightened, then reached for a crutch. "You wouldn't—Naw, you're just razzin' me. You wouldn't trick an old man with a heart condition, would ya, boy?"

"I wouldn't admit it," Justin replied. "Not when you're holding a weapon.''

Charley grinned at the crutch and shook it threateningly at Justin. "Just you remember it.''

Beth watched with amusement as Charley leaned back and settled the crutch with a disgruntled thump. Justin knew how to handle the old curmudgeon. Funny how quickly he'd settled himself into the household. Now, just when it was starting to feel comfortable, that would change, she thought. She watched with a sinking feeling as Justin mounted the stairs, feeling his way, never taking his eyes from the pages in his hand. Already, his world intruded on hers. But what else could she expect? Although he didn't know it, she wouldn't have much of a world left if it weren't for this consulting bit. Most likely, she'd be in bankruptcy court.

Charley's voice broke into her thoughts, preventing her from dwelling on her problems. "Here, make yourself useful and help me to the kitchen. I hear Eva settin' the food onto the table.'' Then he shouted for Justin, roaring in Beth's ear until she threatened to clobber him with his own crutch.

Beth was quiet during the midday meal, but her silence was offset by Justin's excitement over the script as he answered Aunt Eva's questions about the project.

The older woman was shaking her head. "I just don't see how anybody can memorize that much."

"It's a lot of work," Justin said. "But it's easier if I understand the character I'm playing. How he thinks, what his past is, what he hopes for the future."

"Can't be that much to it," Charley grumbled. "Just standing in front of the camera and spouting someone else's words—"

"There's a lot to remember," Aunt Eva interjected. "And actors have to pretend they're feeling things they're not."

"They do it on the news every night. You don't think those people care whether some drunk shot some other drunk, do you? Naw, they just read it off a big board on the wall."

Beth tapped the old man's arm, attempting to distract him before he became too outspoken and offensive, before he drove his blood pressure up too high again. "I was thinking of buying some calves," she said.

"I hope you fix the fence first," he retorted, then turned back to Justin. "I'll tell you who had it tough, though, and that's the guy that lived it."

"I agree," Justin said. "That's why I want to do this movie."

Charley waved his fork in midair. "You agree? Well, dammit, nobody'll argue with me anymore. Takes all the joy outta life."

Beth's eyes caught the twinkling amusement in Justin's and she stifled a laugh. "When do you start filming?"

"August twentieth."

She nodded and stared down at her plate; what little appetite she'd had was gone. She hadn't wanted him to come. Now the thought of him leaving cast a pall over the evening.

Justin's knee touched hers under the table, and she edged away, thinking she must be crowding him. When his fingers clasped her leg, she realized it was no accident, and her startled gaze flew to his face. He kept his expression neutral as he continued to discuss the film with Charley and Aunt Eva. And all the while, his hand rested at her knee, stroking the soft, worn denim that might as well not have been there for all the protection it afforded Beth's oversensitive flesh. She'd never realized how many nerves ended at her knee, nerves connected to her tingling spine, her laboring lungs and the tickling, tugging sensation beneath her breastbone.

The feelings distracted her so much that she barely heard his voice, and missed the words altogether.

"What?" she asked. "I'm sorry. I was thinking of something else." She felt herself blush under Justin's knowing glance, and crossed her legs, shifting her knee away from his grasp.

"I asked if you could help me with my lines," he repeated.

"I'm not sure," she said, looking to Aunt Eva for help.

"I just need you to read through the scenes with me and cue me, prompt me when I forget what comes next." It seemed like a reasonable request to him. So why did Beth seem suddenly pale?

"Reading aloud?" she asked with a slight quiver in her voice.

"It works better that way," he replied, then immediately regretted his sarcasm. A flash of panic in her eyes as she gazed at Aunt Eva puzzled him.

"I don't think that would work out," Beth eased her chair back and stood up.

Justin wasn't satisfied with that. "Why not?"

She looked past him, avoiding his eyes. "I'm already behind on the paperwork," she said, then hurried from the room.

Justin watched her go, then turned to the others for an answer. The paperwork was just an excuse, he knew. She spent enough time in that office of hers to do the paperwork for ten farms this size. They'd agreed to go slowly, and he thought that meant allowing time to know each other. This was a prime opportunity, to his way of thinking, but evidently she disagreed.

"I guess I said the wrong thing," he told the others.

Charley opened his mouth to speak, but a stern look from Aunt Eva stopped him, and instead he shoved a bite of potatoes in. At that moment, Justin felt the rejection more deeply than any he could remember. All of them had closed ranks against him. He hadn't felt this much an outsider since he went home last Christmas—when his designer clothes and shiny Ferrari had set him apart from his family. The problem was him, not them. He was the outsider, and he didn't know how to bridge the gap.

It was nearly dark before Justin saw Beth again. He and Aunt Eva were huddled close at the kitchen table, sharing the single copy of the script when Beth trudged into the kitchen in her sock feet. Her clothes were grimy, and bits of straw dropped out of the rolled cuffs of her jeans. For a moment, she listened quietly to Aunt Eva's deadpan recitation of the words before her, contrasting sharply with Justin's impassioned reading of his lines. He stopped midsentence when he noticed her, his pretend scowl fading into a tentative smile.

"You just get back?" Aunt Eva queried.

Beth shook her head. "About an hour ago."

The older woman's brows arched suspiciously. "I didn't hear the truck."

Beth glanced pointedly at the script. "I guess you were busy." She reached into the cabinet for a glass and filled it with tap water.

"Ross usually stops in at the house for a piece of my pie," Aunt Eva said with a mildly accusing stare at her niece. "Didn't you ask him in?"

Beth looked away. "He had to get home to feed the stock."

"You bought the calves?" Justin asked, keeping his expression neutral. "Or did Ross buy something?"

"I bought four," she answered. "We put them in the back pasture with Witch, and triple-wired the gate. With any luck, Witch won't take them on a tour of the neighborhood anytime soon."

"Brownie wasn't looking too good today," Aunt Eva interjected. "Justin put her up in the barn where we could watch her."

Beth nodded. "Ross and I had a look at her. He thinks I out to put her down, but I just can't do it yet. I know she's old, but she doesn't seem to be in any pain." She took another large swallow of water and turned her attention to Justin. "Did you and the boys get the barn cleaned out?"

He nodded. "Didn't take long. I put them to work out in the tomatoes, tying up the plants and weeding. That's what Charley suggested." He allowed himself a wry smile at the thought of Charley *suggesting* anything. The old grouch had barked out orders right and left all afternoon. He'd followed them around on his crutches until Aunt Eva had threatened him with a rolling pin and a long hospital stay if he didn't return to the house.

Beth's raised brows indicated she thought there was more to the story than Justin was telling, but she simply nodded and said, "Good" before heading for the doorway.

"Wait," he said, continuing when she turned her attention back onto him. "The old tractor is running a bit rough. I thought I'd take a look at it tomorrow."

"Which one?"

"The old Cub."

"Let Charley look at it," she said. "He's been working on the Cub for years. He's a pretty decent mechanic."

So am I, Justin added silently as he watched her wander slowly through the entryway and out of sight, her hips swaying enticingly beneath the grimy denim. Even covered with dust, smelling of cow sweat and worse, she was sexy as hell. And he had a quick mental flash of green silk blowing aside to reveal delicate pink garters and soft white skin.

As he and Aunt Eva resumed reading, he spoke with only half his attention on the words before him. The other half followed the squeak of the hall floorboards beneath Beth's feet, the rushing sound of the water in the bathroom as she scrubbed up, and the inevitable thump of the office door closing behind her.

The latter was symbolic, he thought several times over the course of the next few days. Something seemed to be bothering her, but she'd shut him out. She'd been warm and soft against him the other day in the delivery truck, and her flesh had trembled beneath his touch. He'd caught her twice, watching him with wide, wanting eyes, and he'd answered with a hungry look of his own. Indecision had hovered in her expression before she turned away. He felt he was losing her before she was ever his. And he didn't know how to recapture the magic that had been growing between them.

He couldn't understand, either, why it mattered so much to him. For years, one woman had been much the same as the next. Oh, some were prettier, some smarter, but none of them affected him deeply. He hadn't let them. But Beth reminded him too much of Carla, his high school girlfriend. His brother's wife now. But she'd been Justin's only love until their dreams separated them. She wanted a home, children, and security in the familiar neighborhood where they'd both grown up. And he wanted to escape it.

He hadn't realized then that he couldn't escape who he was. Or that someday he would no longer want to.

Justin had just about come to terms with his feelings for Beth by the time he returned late Friday morning from the usual round of deliveries. She'd kept her distance, but sometimes there was a new wistfulness in her expression—such as on this morning when she'd closed the truck door behind the last crate and waved him out of the yard.

Justin parked the truck and stowed the empty crates in the shed, then headed for the house with an armful of takeout food. For two days, he and Beth had eaten cold sandwiches and yogurt. Since Aunt Eva and Charley wouldn't be home until Saturday, Justin had taken defensive measures.

Eva had taken Charley into the city for a round of

tests, a new walking cast, and a lesson in rehabilitation therapy.

"I pity the nurse stuck with him," Justin muttered as he set the containers on the kitchen counter. Except for a smear of peanut butter and a few breadcrumbs, the counter gleamed as cleanly as it had when Aunt Eva left early that morning.

"At least I know she's already had lunch," he muttered as he shuffled through the containers. With Aunt Eva gone for two days, meals would be a chancy thing, so he'd picked up an assortment of takeout on the way home. His cooking skills were minimal, and Beth never did more than throw together a sandwich. At least this way, they'd have a little variety this weekend.

Half an hour later, he found Beth in the big old barn, cursing loudly at the disassembled tractor parts scattered around her in the dusty straw. The tractor itself was parked a few feet away in the wide aisle between the stalls. She grabbed up a yellowed booklet and bent over the engine, staring from one to the other before she set the booklet aside and reached for a wrench. She banged around a bit in the engine, then dropped back down to her knees and traced a grimy finger around the exploded diagram on the page.

"Whoever drew these pictures must have flunked out of art school," she muttered.

"I think the engineers do the exploded drawings for the manuals. Which might explain why they're so hard to read," Justin said from behind her, startling her so that she dropped the wrench. It left a greasy trail across her jeans and landed in the dust.

"You have an irritating habit of sneaking up on people," she grated out as she reached for the tool and struggled to control the blue language that threatened to slip past her lips any second. "Why don't you take up whistling or something so I'll have some warning."

Justin scowled down at the mess she'd made of the engine. "What happened?"

"It quit when I was plowing under the spring brassicas this morning."

"And?"

"The boys and I towed it up here." Her frown deepened. "And I can't even figure out what piece does what, let alone what's wrong. I suspect Charley's jerry-rigged this thing, like he's done everything else around here. For all I know, this could be off the old lawn mower," she added, holding up the distributor cap.

Justin squinted down at it. "Not likely."

She looked doubtfully at him, not knowing whether he'd be more help or hindrance.

"Do you have any old newspapers?" he asked.

"What for?" she asked, puzzled by the odd request.

"To spread this stuff out on. All this dirt will do more damage than whatever the original problem was. And you won't be as likely to lose any small parts in the straw."

"Good idea," she answered, not moving. "I think Aunt Eva keeps the old papers in the garage." Then she turned her attention back to the diagram, and dragged over a book he hadn't noticed before, a thick volume with torn and stained pages and a well-worn cover.

"I guess this means I'm getting the newspapers," he said. The only answer was a snort from Brownie as the old horse bumped against the stall door behind him.

Beth was gone when Justin returned a few minutes later, so he set to work without her. By the time she returned, he was close to figuring out the problem, although he knew it would take a bit of time to correct it.

An off-key whistle heralded her approach, and he shot her a pained look. The twinkling in her eyes distracted him for a moment before he forced himself to turn back to the dismantled engine. "The points are fouled," he said.

"Oh. Then it's not serious."

"Not really. It shouldn't take the two of us long to get it running again," he said, then gave her directions on how to help him.

Actually, it took longer than he'd expected, mostly because Beth kept arguing about what part went where. It had been a long time, he had to admit, since he'd helped his dad at the city maintenance shed, and he'd evidently forgotten a few things. However, when the last bolt was threaded into place, he smiled and turned the key.

Nothing happened. He tried again, but still heard nothing more than the click of the ignition key with no power behind it.

"Why didn't you tell me the battery was dead?" he asked.

"It wasn't this morning," Beth said, brows knit in puzzlement. "The Cub started fine. It ran a little rough, but I guess that must have been the points. Charley keeps a spare battery charged up in the garage. I'll get it."

By the time she returned, Justin had removed the dead battery.

"I tested it. This one's fully charged," she said as she handed the battery over. Working together, they slipped the charged one into place, then connected it. But the tractor still wouldn't start.

"You're going to have to help me," he told Beth as he tried the key for the third time. "Start reading that checklist at the top of the page. Maybe I can figure it out with your help. Tell me what the book says while I look over the engine."

"What?" A panicked expression replaced the calm, matter-of-fact demeanor she'd worn since he'd first picked up the wrench that afternoon.

"The thick book, *Basic Engine Repair*. It's right over there." He pointed vaguely in the direction of the book, lying closed with several strands of straw marking the place. "Read me the part that starts right after the photo at the top."

Beth hesitated, then grabbed a wrench. "You read. I'll work."

Justin held up his grease-smeared hands. "Yours are cleaner."

"I could get one of the boys," she suggested, dropping the wrench and backing away uncertainly.

Frowning, Justin searched Beth's uncomfortable expression for a clue to the real reason she'd suddenly changed her mind about working with him. If he'd made a pass, he'd understand. Difficult as it had been, he hadn't touched her, not even when her top button fell open and exposed the shadow between her breasts.

"What's wrong?" he demanded.

"Nothing. I just thought of something I need to do."

Justin wasn't buying it. This wasn't the first time she'd turned cold and panicky for no apparent reason. Only this time, he intended to find out what he'd done, what he'd said, to force such a change in her.

"What's the real problem?" he pressed.

She shrugged and strolled over to Brownie's stall,

answering the mare's hoarse whicker with a vigorous scratch between her fuzzy ears.

She didn't want to tell him that she was terrified of reading aloud, that she'd never graduated from high school because until recently she couldn't read at all. She didn't want him to know she studied every night to prepare for the equivalency test.

"Like I said, I forgot to do something."

"What's that?" His voice came from right behind her. Funny how she hadn't heard him move. He was simply there.

She stilled, holding her breath until Brownie nudged her hard, begging for more attention. She spun around and studied Justin's resolute expression. He expected an answer, and a good one this time. Well, he wasn't going to get it.

"I'll be back in a little while," she said. "I'll send one of the boys down."

"Don't bother," Justin said, glaring at her. Then she whirled and stalked down the wide passageway, feeling his eyes bore into her back with every step. It was a relief to round the corner, but she felt the shame more deeply. She headed for the gardens and attacked the weeds with a frenzy until the shame and frustration faded, replaced by a familiar physical weariness.

The sun was settling close to the horizon when Beth returned to the barn to feed and water the animals. Justin didn't even glance her way. She knew it was no less than she deserved. She could have tried to help him. She shouldn't be so self-conscious, so touchy about the issue. She was too old for those kinds of games.

She'd just emptied the uneaten feed from Brownie's bucket and replaced it with fresh oats when the tractor sputtered to life behind her. It hesitated, then chugged smoothly, filling the barn with a cloud of exhaust. Justin climbed into the seat and disappeared down the driveway for a test drive while Beth finished the chores.

A few minutes later, Justin parked the tractor and joined her. "All fixed?" she asked.

He nodded. "It was just a short, a grounded wire. Go on inside. I'll finish up here," he said, taking the bucket from her. Nodding her agreement, she left, walking with slow, dejected steps.

A bit later, Justin found Beth elbow-deep in suds in the downstairs bathroom, scrubbing away the worst of the grime. "She's running good now," he commented, laughing at Beth's arched brow.

"That tractor is definitely a 'he.' A lot of noise and a lot of trouble," she retorted, trying to hide the wave of relief that washed through her at his improved mood. She rinsed off quickly and stepped aside, reaching for a towel. Her hands stilled when she saw the smoky, smoldering look in Justin's eyes as they caught hers, then darted lower.

"Button your blouse, Beth," he said hoarsely.

She glanced down and gasped, spinning around as her fingers nimbly slid not one, but two miscreant buttons back into place.

"I'll start supper," she muttered, slipping out into the hall.

"Don't bother. I got something in town. It's all in the refrigerator. Take your pick."

As Beth stared at the array of takeout containers spread over the countertop a few minutes later, she had to stifle the urge to giggle. "You weren't afraid of starving, were you?" she asked him when he finally made his way to the kitchen. He'd changed from his grease-stained clothes into a clean pair of snug-fitting jeans and blue pullover a shade darker than his eyes.

His sheepish grin took the insult out of his words. "I couldn't eat another tomato sandwich. I wasn't sure what kind of junk food you like, so I got a good selection. Shall we start with the nachos?"

Beth lifted the container of chips that had gone soggy from the cheese and too many peppers. "Sounds like torture," she said, then peeked in the other containers.

They settled on a sampling of pizza, Chinese, and Chef Roberto's golden beet experiment. "Not bad," Beth said after tasting the rich concoction. "I'll bet it's really good served fresh and hot."

Justin's reaction was more noncommittal. Despite his outward good humor, he seemed wary and a bit tense, although he'd kept up his end of the banter while they ate.

"Something bothering you?" she finally asked.

He studied her for an instant, then shook his head. "Just trying to figure you out. Every time I think I know who you are, you change. Like this afternoon."

"Marlene always said a woman shouldn't be too predictable or she'd bore a man," Beth quipped lightly, though her eyes avoided his.

"Somehow I don't think you really care," Justin replied, leaning back in his chair.

Beth toyed with the Chinese noodles on her plate for a moment before speaking. "I think it's better not to."

"What really happened this afternoon? Do you hate being around me that much?" he asked, his voice roughening.

Beth's startled glance fell on his pained expression. Instead of anger, she recognized the sad vulnerability that was so unexpected it tore at her heart. She'd hurt him, and she found the thought unbearable.

"Just the opposite," she admitted, holding his gaze.

"Then why couldn't you stand to work with me?"

"It wasn't you. It was me," she said, debating how much to tell him. "I don't like to read aloud. That's why I didn't want to help you anymore."

"Why didn't you say so?" he replied in an exasperated tone. "It's no big deal."

A brief, hard laugh escaped Beth's lips before she pursed them into a frown. "It *is* a big deal," she argued. "I stumble over the words and sometimes the letters get all jumbled up."

Justin waved a hand deprecatingly in the air. "Don't be ridiculous. You're making more out of this than you should."

His dismissive attitude angered her. It reminded her of all the thoughtless people who had acted the same way, people who absorbed the words almost as easily as they breathed. They couldn't comprehend the difficulties she had overcome just to get a driver's license.

"I'm not being ridiculous or melodramatic or overly sensitive," she retorted. "I didn't even graduate from high school. I'm what they call a dyslexic." She'd learned at the special school not to be ashamed of it, or she thought she had. She'd learned to cope with it, how to unjumble the letters and make sense out of them. But old habits and taunting memories died hard, and she still remembered how stupid she'd felt.

"You?" He seemed surprised.

"It's true. Ask Charley. Ask Aunt Eva. Ask my mother. I didn't even know I had dyslexia until after Marlene married Alfred. I just thought I was dumb, and so did everybody else until Alfred hired a tutor, then sent me to a school that specializes in people with learning disorders.''

"So that's why you wouldn't help me with the script."

"I don't like reading in front of people," she repeated. "It's awkward. I'm still not very good."

"You've come a long way since high school," he said, smiling as if her disclosure didn't make a whit of difference.

"That's just it," she said. "I really haven't. If the farm went under, I'd end up waiting tables or cleaning rooms in some motel. You can't do much else without a high school diploma."

"You could get your G.E.D."

She smiled patronizingly.

"I guess you've heard that before," he added.

She nodded. "You didn't really think I was doing paperwork for the farm every night, did you? I've been studying."

"I thought you were avoiding me."

She shook her head. "Not really."

"Why didn't you say something? I would have helped you study. Heck, you could have saved me from Charley's cutthroat card games."

"I was ashamed," she admitted. "Aunt Eva's really the one who's held this place together. She handles the accounts, the bills, tells me how I need to price my produce."

"Your aunt's getting old. She won't always be able to help you."

Beth sighed, then stood, taking her plate to the sink. "I know. That's why I've been studying." As they put the leftovers away, she didn't mention the mistakes the older woman had made, or her failing eyesight. That wasn't her confession to make.

"I think I'll go check on the irrigation pump. The boys said the pond is about dry now. Tomorrow we'll have to move it over to the lake," she said, with a worried frown.

Unexpectedly, Justin leaned closer, lightly kissing the lines before smoothing them away with his thumbs. As the slumberous warmth spread through her, she swayed closer. But before his lips could touch hers, the alarm bells in her head jangled, pulling her back.

"Beth?" His hands cupped her face, holding her for his kiss. He touched lightly, teasing and tempting, enough to heat the desire sleeping in the pit of her belly, and lower. But not enough to frighten her, to threaten her.

And when his head lifted she was trembling. They both were. "Beth?" he questioned, though they both knew what he was really asking.

She shook her head. "I'd better check the pump," she said huskily. "Alone."

EIGHT

A deep rumble of thunder awakened Beth from an uneasy sleep. For a moment she lay there, feeling sticky and hot in the humid air and longing for the air-conditioned comfort of Marlene's penthouse.

"I hope this isn't another false promise," she murmured, talking as much to the clouds above the roof as to herself.

She waited a while, listening to the whispering rustle of the leaves and staring at the eerie shadows cast on the wall by the intermittent flashes of lightning. When the wind picked up, billowing the curtains out until they flapped and brushed against the coverlet of her bed, she pushed herself upright.

"I must be crazy," she muttered, then groaned at the aching crick in her neck. Independence had its drawbacks, she thought. There were advantages to being a kept woman, air-conditioning, spas with masseuses, no midnight vigils waiting for rain that never falls.

Dangerous thoughts. Resolutely, she pushed them away and slammed her window shut.

She fumbled around in the dark for a minute for her robe, then gave up the search. The oversize nightshirt she wore hid everything from her neck to her knees anyway. Pulling it on, she headed across the hall to check the other bedrooms. That finished, she halted outside Justin's door and raised her hand to knock. But her knuckles never touched the wood-paneled door. Instead, they trembled on her lips as she remembered the toe-curling kiss in the kitchen only hours before. No, she'd not tempt herself by rousing him in the middle of the night, even if it meant water stains on the polished wood floor when the rain blew in.

If it truly rained. Twice before this month, lightning had split the night sky around them, but the clouds blew away, leaving no more than a few scattered drops in the dust. Nevertheless, she traipsed downstairs just in case. She didn't relish the thought of polishing that many floors.

The front door stood wide open and Beth hurried to close it, berating herself for not locking it earlier. Before she touched the handle to close it, a flash of lightning outlined Justin's figure on the porch steps.

Beth felt like the lightning had hit her, so strong was her body's response to the mere sight of him. Her skin tingled and her nipples hardened so that even the soft nap of the nightshirt felt like an erotic caress as she shifted from foot to foot. And beneath her breasts, her chest tightened, squeezing her breath from her. The butterflies beneath her ribs fluttered, then crowded into a dense, vibrating cluster that sank into the pit of her stomach and lower still.

She knew she ought to turn and run back upstairs and bolt her door. But against what? Against her own traitorous emotions? Against temptation?

An eerie glow from the yard light stopped just short of the porch, blocked by the thick leaf cover of the old maple trees. Beth studied Justin's tense pose, trying to decide whether to join him or creep upstairs and leave well enough alone.

Before she could decide, it was decided for her. Heaving a deep sigh, Justin turned and glimpsed her, a pale shadow in the doorway. His eyes met hers. Midnight eyes, barely visible in the darkness, they captured her as surely as if she'd walked into a cage.

"I didn't know you were up," she said from her side of the screen.

He twisted around, glancing over his shoulder at the sky. "I couldn't sleep," he said. His tone was surprisingly normal, not the low, sexy growl she'd expected after the look he'd just given her. No, he hadn't captured her. She'd captured herself.

"The thunder woke me, too. Do you think it'll really rain this time?" She stepped out onto the porch as she spoke, settling into a cushioned wicker chair and pulling the long shirt down over her knees. *Think of normal things and normality will return.*

"God only knows," he answered. "But just in case, I closed all the windows, except yours. I didn't want to disturb you."

She smiled, remembering how she'd crept away from his door a moment ago. A bright flash, followed immediately by a bone-shaking crash of thunder erased the smile.

"That hit somewhere close," she said, jumping to her feet and leaning over the porch rail, searching the shadows uneasily. It would be just her luck for lightning to set fire to the barn, or golf-ball size hail to pound her crops into the mud. She needed rain, but a soft, gentle, life-giving rain.

The porch floor creaked behind her as Justin's hand settled on her shoulder. "It was a few miles away. Not close enough to be your problem."

"It's somebody's problem," she reminded him.

"Probably the kale farm," Justin teased. "It hit the middle of the field and set fire to the entire crop. And you'll once again be furious with me, because I indirectly caused the disaster by praying for rain and dancing under a full moon." He added an exaggerated sniff and whimper for effect.

She smirked at his melodramatics. "Quit feeling sorry for yourself. You didn't know what you were doing back then. It was your first day. I've all but forgotten it."

His fingers began to work on the stiff muscles in her shoulders. "You're awfully tense. Is it because of me?" he asked baldly.

If anything, her spine stiffened even more. "Why would you think that?"

"I pushed you pretty hard today. Enough to make you nervous about being alone with me like this." When she didn't answer, he leaned closer, his breath tickling her ear. "Are you nervous?"

"I'm thirsty," she said, pulling away. "Shall I get you something, too?" She couldn't see his expression in the darkness but was sure he wore a self-satisfied smile. He'd provoked a reaction, and she'd answered him as clear as if she'd shouted "yes."

A few minutes later, she handed Justin a tall glass of fruit juice. He leaned back in the chair he'd taken and tilted his glass to his lips. Taking a single sip from her own glass, she set it aside and descended the steps, holding her hands out, palms facing upward. The wind had eased as the thunderheads blew past them and rumbled in the distance. The air felt heavy and humid, and even the crickets were silent.

She stepped out into the grass, beyond the circle of trees.

"Anything yet?" Justin called as he followed her. She felt one drop, then two. Then a large splatter hit her nose. She turned her face skyward as the drops thickened and pattered around her, on her. Within seconds, the clouds unleashed a downpour, drenching her hair and soaking her nightshirt until both were plastered against her skin. She closed her eyes, turning blindly in circles in a laughing dance of gratitude for the crop-saving rain.

It was happening! The drought was over, and with it the hours and hours of daily watering and shifting irrigation equipment, of worrying whether the old pump would die and whether the pond levels would sink too low.

When she stopped spinning and opened her eyes, Justin was there, his hands reaching out to steady her as she swayed dizzily.

"It's raining," she told him inanely.

He matched her silly grin with one of his own. "Just a little." His hands trembled on her arms. Then his fingers trailed upward, leaving a burning path along her forearm until they slipped under the clinging T-shirt to grasp her shoulders.

Still brimming with the exhilaration of her laughing rain dance, she leaned into the embrace, linking her own fingers in his hair and pulling his lips closer.

He stopped, inches away, tantalizing her with the nearness, with the hard press of his body against her own. Time stood still for that moment, then splintered into a thousand disjointed fragments as their lips came together in a very different sort of dance.

Beth felt boneless, all heat and soft, sensuous flesh with no starch to hold her upright. As her knees weakened and bent, Justin lifted her to him, sliding her body boldly up his own until their eyes were on a level. She wrapped her legs around him, clinging to him like she'd clung to high-branched trees as a child. Except that there was nothing childlike or innocent in what she was feeling. Although the warning bells pealed in her brain, her body was awakening to sensations she'd never imagined.

When the raindrops formed a trickle down his temple, she kissed the moisture away, then followed the path upward with the tip of her tongue. Gasping, he sank to his knees, taking them both to the wet grass.

Beth felt the strength, the power of her desire surge through her as she touched him. Love made her strong in unimagined ways, spiritual ways, and she savored the idea. Her lips tasted his neck, while his fingertips kneaded her shoulders, then trailed lower to her swelling breasts. Where the fabric clung, he pushed it aside, sinking down until he sat on the ground beneath her, with her legs still circling him.

"This is crazy," he said, arching to grant her greater access to the sensitive side of his neck.

"Why?" she whispered, pulling back to see his face, his eyes. She couldn't read him, but she could feel his frantic heartbeat beneath her fingertip. He was as affected as she was, maybe more, she thought, suddenly conscious of the fullness she lay against. She felt good, too good, and wondered why she'd never known this exhilaration before.

"Making love in the grass, in the rain," he gasped when she shifted away, and his firm hand pulled her back against him as he continued in a rough, gravelly voice. "Sitting in a puddle in the yard when there's a perfectly good bed in the house."

Beth leaned back, arching her brows provocatively. Then the full import of what she was doing struck her, the irrevocable crossing of boundaries. "Oh?" she whispered. The single syllable conveyed all that she was at that moment in resonant tones that struck at Justin's heart.

"Yes, oh. You can't kiss me, touch me like that, and just leave me sitting in the mud," he answered. His finger trailed the length of her leg, stopping high on the inside of her thigh. Beth felt the quivering heat and locked away the doubts.

"Are you asking or telling?"

His hand dropped away. He leaned back, considering, bracing himself on outstretched arms until they touched only at the hip. The glow of the yard light cast a silvery light across the handsome planes of his face, now set in serious lines. His shirt was unbuttoned and pulled free at the waist where she'd run her fingers up over bare flesh.

"Asking," he finally said, though he looked at her as if once she decided, there was no turning back on either path.

She hesitated, then uncurled herself from his lap and stood, unconscious of the provocative cling of the wet nightshirt. When she held out her hand to him, an answering flame flickered in his eyes before he took it and let her pull him upright.

"Is that a yes?" he asked.

She stood on tiptoe and kissed the underside of his

chin, teasing his chest with her fingertips. "You couldn't tell?"

"I want to be sure. I want *you* to be sure. No regrets. No tears. No shame."

She nodded. There was no shame in what she was feeling. She couldn't promise there wouldn't be regrets or tears in time, but there would be none tonight. And if they came in the weeks after he returned to California, she'd deal with what she'd done as best she could.

"I want this," she said, her voice sure and strong. "I want you."

Yet he led her slowly to her antique brass bed in the room that had witnessed the love of her grandparents, the birth of her mother, and the death of her grandfather before she'd been born herself. And if there were ghosts there, they were silent, recognizing the feelings that were almost tangible between Beth and Justin.

There was eagerness, passion in the taking, but the slow savoring made the feelings that much more intense. Justin touched and teased, then retreated, coaxing Beth's body to a fever pitch while he murmured love words to entrance her soul.

Following her instincts, Beth touched back, exploring the lean, muscled shoulders that had first warned her this man was more than she had anticipated. She let her hands venture lower, caressing without shyness what she had not seen, what she saw now only in the pale flashes of lightning that the curtains could not block. And then her eyes closed as the pleasure intensified, as he touched between her legs and stroked her heated flesh until neither could wait any longer. Beth stiffened as he entered her, expecting pain and feeling none. And then there was only pleasure, so intense she thought she'd burst.

Sometime afterward, as the first tendrils of dawn lightened the sky, a cool breeze across her bare skin awakened Beth. She slitted her eyelids to watch Justin, standing naked before the open window, staring pensively into space. Before she could think to call him back to her, she drifted back to sleep.

When she next awoke, it was broad daylight. She turned over to snuggle against the man sleeping next to her. Only he wasn't sleeping. He was wide-awake, very awake, and his fingers were stirring needs she thought had been well taken care of the night before. When she moaned, he pulled back.

"Sore?"

"Barely," she whispered, and reached for him.

Afterward, she lay thinking that it was a good thing no deliveries were scheduled that day. Because it was long past time for the truck to leave. As it was, she could enjoy the sated closeness, savor it, and save it in her mind for when she was once again alone. It wasn't until she heard the crunch of tires on gravel that she bestirred herself to rise. A sputtering backfire warned that her young employees had arrived.

"Stay a while longer," Justin said, taking her arm and pulling her back down to the mattress. The bedsprings creaked as he shifted, trapping her beneath him.

"We have to get to work," she said. "Charley and Aunt Eva could come back at any time. Besides, the boys are here."

"I think they can find something to keep them busy for a while. I want to ask you something."

She could tell by his expression that this was serious. The grin had faded, replaced by a hint of vulnerability.

"Why?" he asked her.

"What do you mean, why? Why what?"

"Why me?"

Beth forced a grin that was in sharp contradiction with the uneasy churning of her insides. "Why not you?"

Justin rolled away, reaching for his pants. "That's not an answer."

"What do you want me to say? That you're sexy. That you have nice eyes. You already know that. That's why they pay you the big bucks."

He dropped the jeans on the bed and sat down. "I want the truth. You're not the type to make love lightly or to fall for the outside package. And unless I'm greatly mistaken, you've never done this before."

Beth pulled the twisted sheet up, covering herself as best she could. "I'd hoped it didn't show quite so plainly." *He regretted it,* she thought. *Already he wished he hadn't touched her. He thought he'd taken a sexy, earthy woman to bed, and discovered she was a virgin.* She willed the knife twisting between her ribs to stop, but the pain continued, a physical pain for a heartfelt injury.

Justin sighed and pulled her resisting body close. "Except for one particular moment," he whispered, "I wouldn't have known it. It was the most fantastic, most erotic experience of my life. I wish it would rain every night."

A tense laugh escaped Beth's lips as relief spilled through her. She wanted to believe him, to trust her instincts. "Aunt Eva would have kittens if she had seen us like that on the lawn," she said in a shaky voice.

"She'd be jealous. Next thing you know she'd be dragging Charley out into the rain, cast and all."

Beth reluctantly smiled at the incongruous picture in her mind. "Not in a million years," she said.

"They don't know what they're missing," he said.

"Then you're not sorry? Or disappointed?"

"No." He pressed a kiss to her nape. "But you didn't answer my question. Why me?"

Beth drew a deep breath, but it didn't help. "I don't know. I never felt—" she flung her arms out helplessly.

"Love? Is it love?" he asked, his dulcet tone gloving the demand that she answer truthfully.

When she nodded, he kissed her, not like before, not urgently or with wild passion, but with a sense of promise that brought tears to her eyes.

"I knew it would be this way," he told her. "From that first night, I knew it would be good between us. It just took me a while to convince you."

"I've wasted a lot of time. There's not much left," she said.

Lightly brushing the curve of her cheek, he smiled. "We have years to get to know one another."

"I wish we did, but the contract is up in a few weeks. You'll start filming and then one movie will follow another."

"You could come back with me."

"What about my farm? I can't just leave in the middle of summer, my busiest season. Then there's Charley and—"

He stopped her panicked tirade with his lips. Each time she tried to pull back, to voice yet another protest, he held her, kissing her until she relented, and returned his kisses with equal fervor.

"You're special. You're different," he whispered in her ear between kisses. "*This* is special."

Beth's heart captured the words, sorted them, and clung to the ones that tripped her heartbeat, throwing an erratic skip into even the pattern and sending warmth through her body. *You're special.*

But it was the other words that stuck in her mind, that epitomized their relationship. *You're different.* A country innocent who engaged in the very unglamorous profession of farming. A fool, too, if she believed the novelty wouldn't fade. She only hoped it didn't fade too quickly. But perhaps it was already. Noticeably absent from his suggestions was the possibility of filming at least part of *Nebraska Sunrise* at Thompson Farm. He'd offered the impossible because he knew she couldn't accept.

Her smile was sad when she spoke again. "Do you ever get bored here? It's pretty tame compared to what you must be used to."

"You think Charley's tame? And those crazy animals of yours? This place is a circus compared to my house."

"You know what I mean. Living here is a lot different from a big city."

His expression was serious as he considered. "I don't miss California, if that's what you mean. I don't miss the traffic or the fourteen-hour days at the studio or the phony smiles at the boring parties. I haven't enjoyed that kind of life for a long time, but I didn't know how to change. It's easy to get swallowed up and lose sight of reality."

"You're an actor," she said. "Illusions and fantasies are your business."

He shook his head. "It's not me anymore. I've felt more grounded, more alive in the last few weeks than I have for several years. I don't think three more weeks will be enough," he said.

She touched his lips. "Let's take it a day at a time for now."

He started to speak, hesitated, then kissed her lightly on the shoulder. "Have it your way for now," he said. "What shall we do today?"

Beth glanced wryly at the clock. "Take a quick shower and then get to work. If we don't show our faces pretty soon, the boys will come looking for us. As it is, we'll be the talk of the county."

"Does that bother you?"

Beth snorted. "Hardly. I've been the talk of the county one way or another all my life. That poor little Thompson girl whose daddy ran off and left her, whose mama spent more time in a cocktail lounge than with her daughter. That woman who thinks she can do a man's job. I just don't want to hurt Ross's feelings."

A frown crossed Justin's features. "He'll survive."

"Of course he will, but he might not forgive me for disillusioning him," she said. "He has this crazy idea that I'm the epitome of good womanhood or something like that."

"Is he in love with you?"

She shook her head. "He's still in love with his wife. I guess I'm just a lot like her."

"I feel sorry for the guy, but I don't want to waste time thinking about him just now," Justin said. "Race you to the shower. Last one there has to cook breakfast."

Beth shrugged and sagged back onto the pillows. "Big deal. There's plenty of leftovers in the fridge. Just hurry up. And don't use all the hot water."

Despite Beth's best intentions, it was another hour before they left the house. A lanky youth met them halfway across the yard.

Beth cast an uncomfortable look at Justin, then stared hard at the boy, almost daring him to remark on the lateness of the hour or the fact that she'd obviously been alone in the house with Justin. But the boy was too upset to notice much.

"You'd better come to the barn quick," he said. "Brownie's down. She looks really bad."

A shaft of fear shot through Beth. "Is she—She's not dead, is she?"

"No. She's having some sort of spasm. It's awful, like she's having a heart attack," he said as he turned and hurried back to the barn, with Beth and Justin close behind.

It took a few seconds for Beth's eyes to adjust to the dimness, but even without looking, she knew something was drastically wrong with the horse. As she passed through the wide doorway, she could hear Brownie's weak thrashings, the irregular thump of hooves against the wall. The two other teenagers stood at the stall door, wide-eyed and helpless.

"You want me to call Doc Dixon?" one asked.

Beth peered into the stall and shook her head. She knew what had to be done. She'd known this day was coming for a long time. Brownie was nearly twenty years old, long past her prime, past even the barest sense of usefulness. Only sentiment had prevented Beth from having her put to sleep.

She sent one of the boys to the house for the hypodermic needle and the vial she'd gotten from Ross for this purpose. While she waited, she stroked the old horse's neck, crooning softly. When the boy returned, she administered the injection and waited for the pain-glazed eyes to close.

And when it was over, she stood and walked straight

into Justin's arms, clutching him tightly, drawing on his strength.

"Are you okay?" he asked.

She nodded against his chest and released him. "I think I'll go for a walk now," she said, only the barest trace of a tremor in her voice, though her eyes shimmered with unshed tears. "Call Ross now. He'll know what to do." She walked out of the barn, refusing to look back at the still, brown body. Justin knew she wanted to be alone. But he found it hard not to run after her and pull her back into his arms and stroke away the grief.

He found her, hours later, after the trucks, the backhoe, and the well-meaning neighbors had left. She sat in the shade next to the lake, tossing acorns into the water. A faint red puffiness around her eyes was the only remaining sign of her tears.

"They buried her in the lower pasture, near the woods," he said, easing himself to the ground beside her and draping an arm across her shoulders. "Charley picked a spot down by the highway."

She nodded. "When did he and Aunt Eva get back?"

"They pulled in a few minutes after you left the barn. I was still trying to track Ross down. Charley took over and had everything arranged within a few minutes."

She chuckled. "Good thing they weren't an hour earlier."

He squeezed her shoulder, then stood up, pulling her with him. "Now I know you're okay."

"What did you think I'd do? Drown myself in the lake over a horse?"

"Nothing that drastic," he said. "But you've been gone for several hours. What did you do all that time?"

Still holding his hand, Beth started for the house, tugging lightly until he strolled along beside her. "Walked around. Thought. Told myself I'd never be that selfish again."

"Selfish? What do you mean?"

"I should have put her down months ago. But she didn't seem to be in any pain, and I just couldn't bring myself to do it. I waited too long," she said.

"You couldn't have known this would happen," he said, hoping to reassure her. Her hand tightened on his for a second.

"I should have suspected," she argued. "It's just that I didn't want anything else to change. Brownie is a part of the way things used to be around here when Grandma was alive. I guess it's past time I grew up. I can't stop life from happening."

"Sometimes it's hard to let go," he said.

"Brownie was my best friend when I was a kid. I used to tell her all my troubles," Beth said with a wry laugh.

"You can tell me now," he offered.

She shook her head. "That wouldn't work. You're part of my troubles."

"Well, you have to ask Edgar for advice then," he said, taking her hand again.

Lunch was an uneasy meal with everyone carefully avoiding the subject of Brownie's death. The others discussed the weather until Beth thought she would scream, particularly after Justin winked and nudged her under the table.

"Charley, how's your leg?" she finally asked, hoping to divert the conversation.

"Hurts like hell," he replied. "All that pokin' and proddin' and wrigglin' it this way and that—"

"Don't exaggerate. All they did was change your cast and make you move around a little," Aunt Eva interjected.

Charley shoved a forkful of food into his mouth. "Damned foolishness makes my leg hurt," he muttered.

"But the doctor said—Ooooch." Aunt Eva's admonishment ended in a high squawk, and Beth was stunned to see her aunt flush beet-red. Then the older woman dealt Charley a loud slap. "Keep your hands to yourself, you old boar. I haven't made up my mind yet."

Beth gaped until she noticed Justin's face reddening as he struggled to contain his silent laughter. Clamping her jaw shut, she shot him a warning look.

Beth rolled her eyes. She'd hoped Charley would have mellowed some after a couple of days away, but he was more crotchety than ever. Inactivity didn't set well with him.

"Charley . . ." Justin began, with a quick wink to Beth. "I wonder if you feel up to helping me out this evening."

"You want me to read with you?" The old man nudged Aunt Eva. "We could share, you and me readin' off the same page real cozy-like."

"Sorry, not the script. The director called last night and—"

"You didn't say anything," Beth interrupted.

"I was distracted," he said, eliciting a flaming blush as his eyes reminded her exactly how distracted he'd been. "Anyway, they're making a few changes and I'd rather wait for the revisions before going any further."

"Well, what do you want me to do, then?" Charley demanded.

"The irrigation pump quit yesterday morning," Justin lied smoothly. "I need some help fixing it."

"It was the tractor," Beth said, her brows riding high with puzzlement.

"Old Blue givin' you trouble?" Charley asked, ignoring Beth's comment. "I'll have a look at her."

Justin cleared his throat. "The tractor's fine. Just a bad wire. But I can't get the pump started. It's a good thing it rained last night."

Charley wiped his chin with a crumpled napkin, then eased himself to his feet with the help of the cane that had replaced the crutches. The new walking cast thumped heavy against the hardwood floor as he made his way to the door. "Might as well get to it," he said. "You comin', boy?"

Justin winked again at Beth, then followed Charley out of the house, leaving the two women staring at each other in surprise. Beth wondered, though, how Justin intended to pull off this scam of his.

"That man's a miracle worker," Aunt Eva said. "Getting Charley out of the house is the next best thing to cutting his tongue out."

Beth laughed. "You'd have to get his vocal cords, too, before he'd be quiet. Even then, he'd probably wheeze all day."

"You're right." A smile creased the old woman's face as she began clearing the table.

Although Beth was itching to see whether Justin's ploy worked, she was even more curious about Aunt Eva's slap.

"How was the trip to Kansas City?" Beth asked, thinking she'd lead up to the subject gradually.

Aunt Eva snorted. "That old fool asked me to marry him before we got ten miles down the road. I didn't take him seriously until he grabbed me and kissed me at a rest area.'' She touched her lips, and Beth noticed the smudged traces of what looked like lipstick. Then she saw the darkened brows and lashes and the faint dusting of powder across Aunt Eva's nose.

"You're wearing makeup!'' Beth was stunned. Aunt Eva had never worn makeup.

The older woman smiled tentatively. "Does it look all right?''

Beth eyed her aunt critically. Too much was changing, and she felt a momentary jolt. "It looks good on you. You should have done it a long time ago. Does Charley like it?''

Aunt Eva blushed again and turned away. I guess that answers that, Beth thought. "Are you going to marry him?'' she asked. One more change, and she didn't know whether the thought made her sad or happy. A bit of both, she decided as she waited for Aunt Eva's answer.

"I've been an old spinster for so long, I'm not sure I can change.''

That wasn't what Beth expected. "I suppose Charley can be hard to live with,'' she said.

"Phooey,'' Aunt Eva replied. "He's a lot of hot air. He's a darn good man if you look past the grouchy mouth.''

Beth handed Aunt Eva the last of the dishes from the table and backed away. "Well, I'll leave you to your decision-making and go check on the grouchy mouth and the con artist.''

She found the two of them behind the barn with Charley giving his basic mechanics lecture, while Justin listened intently, pretending he didn't already know the difference between a piston and a spark plug.

"I sure hope you can get this back together," she said, winking over Charley's shoulder. "I'll need it in a week or so."

"Yep, that rain sure helped," Charley said. "Gives us time to give this old thing a good going-over, really put it back into shape."

Heeding Justin's pleading look, she came to his rescue. "Can I borrow your helper? There's a whole list of things that should have been done this morning," she said.

Charley frowned intently at the grimy piece of metal in his hand. "I've managed fine on my own all these years. I'll yell for Eva if I need anything," he said. "Though you could be doin' the man a disservice. He's a quick study. He might've made a decent mechanic if he hadn't taken to show business."

"Maybe we'll be done early," Beth said, noting that Justin already was making his escape.

Once inside the packing shed, the two of them set to work, straightening up and cleaning. Although she'd exaggerated a bit for Charley's sake, there were a few chores to be finished.

"Thanks," she said, pausing for a moment to lean on the broom handle. "I knew Charley needed something to do, but I didn't know how to get him started."

Justin lifted a brow. "I hope he can put it all back together. I jammed one of the pistons, but I think it'll be fine. If Charley doesn't figure it out by the time you need the pump, I'll fix it."

"He can do it." Beth was quite sure of that, but she was surprised at Justin's ingenuity. "It seems there's more to you than I would have guessed."

"Actually," he said, "I used to help my dad at the

city maintenance shed. I've worked on everything from a '57 Chevy to a front-end loader.''

Beth shook her head in surprise. "Beneath all that Hollywood glitter and shine, you have a real blue-collar background, Justin Kyle.''

"I guess you never forget where you came from," he replied with an odd expression on his face.

Puzzled, Beth stared for a moment, then returned to work, wondering what was going on behind those disturbing eyes.

NINE

Beth leaned her elbows on the desk and frowned at the sample test. The sultry, early-August heat, coupled with Justin's presence in the chair opposite her, made concentrating difficult. In the month since she'd confessed her reading problem, he'd spent most evenings in here with her, helping her wade through the study guides and sample tests. And in return, she'd helped him learn his lines, reading haltingly at first, then more easily as the script became so familiar she'd almost memorized it herself.

Beth's hand jerked when the phone rang, leaving a long, jagged pencil streak across the page.

"Keep working, I'll get it," Justin told her when she looked up. He stepped into the hall and picked up the receiver, cutting off the jangling sound in midring.

Beth erased the heavy pencil mark and tried to concentrate on the questions, but her attention kept straying. Judging from Justin's easy laugh and warm tone, it was someone he knew well, Melanie perhaps. Justin's sister called every few days to keep him up to date on her own legal battles and the latest gossip in the business. Beth didn't exactly resent her calls, but they were an uncomfortable reminder that Justin had a whole other life apart from Thompson Farm.

Sighing, she dropped the pencil on the page and closed her eyes. It had been a month since they'd first made love, yet the sound of his voice, a simple touch, could still make her senses purr. The feelings hadn't diminished as she'd expected, but grown stronger. She blushed when she thought of the things they had done together, the places they'd made love.

Lost in sensuous memories, Beth didn't notice when Justin hung up the phone and returned to the room.

"That's enough for this evening," he said, brushing past her to close the book.

"I agree," she said, grinning provocatively. "Let's go for a walk and see if we can find a haystack." The familiar tingle raced along her spine and triggered the fluttering in her midsection as his lips descended to hers.

"The lake path or through the woods?" she asked in a whiskey-rough voice as they drew apart.

His hands ran up and down the length of her arms before grasping her hands. "The driveway," he answered. "We'd better stay out in the open. That's the only way I can be sure we'll talk instead of—of other things."

An icy tongue of unease licked at the heat his kiss had stirred, but she refused to pay any heed. Still, a concerned frown knit her brows as they slipped through the house and out the door.

"Don't look so worried," he told her, tugging at her hand when she hesitated on the porch steps.

"This has something to do with the phone call, doesn't it?" Just that morning, he'd said he planned to stay until he was needed on the *Nebraska* set. That was one more week under the contract, and two beyond that.

"One of the 'Vice Cops' co-stars won't be back and we have to reshoot a couple of scenes for the first fall segment," he explained. "I have to fly back."

Beth frowned. He had to leave. Their time was up. She stiffened her spine and straightened her slumping shoulders. She wouldn't cry or scream or do any of the hysterical things she felt like doing. She'd carry this off with grace and dignity even if it killed her.

"Contract dispute or creative differences?" she asked. How ironic that a show-business ego was derailing her happiness after all, she added silently.

"Mother Nature," Justin said, watching Beth's brows arch in surprise. "The actress who plays my partner's wife is pregnant with twins. She's having problems and her doctor has ordered her to stay in bed for the next three months."

Beth groaned in sympathy for the poor woman. "When do you have to leave?"

Justin winced. "I'm on the ten o'clock flight."

Beth stopped in her tracks, feeling the blood drain from her face. "Ten o'clock," she repeated dumbly. "It's almost seven now."

He backtracked and pulled her into his arms. "You could come with me. I already checked. There's another seat available on the flight."

It was tempting, but she couldn't. There was the G.E.D. test, her responsibilities at the farm, the delivery route, and a hundred other excuses, not the least of which was how much she hated cities.

"I can't," she said.

"I know. The test. But you could come for the weekend. I should be able to finish up by then."

"Why don't you just come back here?"

"Because I want you to see where I live, how I live," he said. "It would mean a great deal to me. Besides, you might even like it there."

And because she couldn't deny him anything when he pleaded with those smoky-blue eyes, she agreed, telling herself she could survive one weekend among the smog and the beautiful people.

"If I can arrange to cover all the bases here," she stipulated.

"You should hire somebody else," he urged. "You're already shorthanded. And in a few weeks I won't be able to spend more than the odd weekend here, at least until the season hiatus."

It was an old argument, and Beth ended it with a slow shake of her head. But her heart lifted somewhat, knowing that at least he wanted to return. At that moment, the thought counted a great deal.

"When will you come back?" she asked.

"Sunday or Monday with you, I hope. I'm not sure. I might have to stick around a couple of days to take care of some other business," he said with the start of a frown.

Old doubts reared their ugly heads again, but she pushed them away. He would come back. He had to. His Jeep was here, along with more luggage than he could pack. More important, she would be here. She had to believe she mattered more to him than the glitz and glitter of the California coast.

"Come on," she said, turning toward the house. "You'd better get packed. I'll drive you to the airport."

He fell into step beside her. As they walked, he mentioned some fence repairs he wanted to make, then moved on to other plans for the farm, some possible and some beyond Beth's means for many years to come. She kept silent, not wanting to spend these last few hours arguing.

And until he boarded the plane, Beth pretended to believe that he'd be part of all these changes. After that, she had only herself to fool, and she didn't think she could be that convincing.

Beth could barely contain her excitement or her nervousness as she rode the elevator to the twelfth floor of the glass-and-steel structure.

She hesitated when the doors swished open, then stepped through the opening into a marble-tiled foyer. Only two doors interrupted the endless reflections of the floor-to-ceiling mirrors. She rang the bell beneath the placard labeled C.J. Schnell.

After a moment, a uniformed woman of indeterminate age opened the door and asked if she was lost.

"I'm here to see Justin," Beth said, in a voice that was decidedly firmer than her knees. "I know I'm early, but I wanted to surprise him."

"You've made a mistake," the stone-faced woman replied. Her tone was as drab as the steel-gray of her hair and the matching cotton work shift and black shoes. "This is the Schnell residence. Now please go or I'll have to call security." She sounded bored, as if she'd heard it all before. Then Beth remembered the phone call she'd made months ago, when she'd tried to contact Justin to accept his offer. This had to be his housekeeper.

"You must be Beatrice. Justin's told me so much

about you,'' Beth said, trying to sound friendlier than she felt.

"Nice try, sweetheart. But this is the Schnell residence. See?" She pointed to the discreet brass placard.

Acting instinctively as the door swung closed, Beth stuck a sleek, spike-heeled foot into the opening. She yelped when the heavy door banged painfully against it. Then the door swung wide to reveal the wrinkled housekeeper clutching a deadly-looking pistol. Looking at her, Beth decided the woman must have been Hitler's grandmother in another life.

"This is crazy," Beth muttered. Just then, the sound of laughter spilled out from a nearby room, and she heard Justin's voice, calling for a toast to celebrate. She wondered then just how big of a surprise this would be for him.

The wise thing to do would be to turn around and leave, find the nearest pay phone and call the apartment. She figured she'd have a fifty-fifty chance of getting Justin on the phone that way. But Beth's temper got the upper hand when a high-pitched giggle interrupted Justin's toast.

"You tell Mr. Carl Justin Schnell, formerly of Danville, Illinois," Beth said, in a low, angry voice, "that if he isn't at the door in two minutes, every reporter in the country will be asking him about the side effects of thunderstorms. And don't forget to mention mosquito bites on parts of him the public hasn't seen."

That said, she whirled and stalked out into the middle of the foyer, flinching as the door slammed shut behind her. Drawing a deep breath, fighting the urge to flee, Beth looked around at the multiple images of herself. The walls reflected an elegant woman, all tailored silk and soft kid leather, with a touch of gold gleaming at her ears and her neck. Her heightened color and the angry sparks in her eyes were the only cracks in the composed picture. But inside she trembled. Inside, she was still an insecure, farm girl who didn't belong here. She wasn't sure who was crazier, the gun-toting housekeeper or herself.

The reflected door behind her opened and Beth's gaze focused on the tall, deceptively dark man framed there.

"You're early," Justin said, walking toward her. It was too dim in the discreetly lit foyer to read his expression, but he seemed like a different man. His black twill pants and black turtleneck matched the stark, colorless sophistication of this place. Only the trailing lock of brown hair on his forehead reminded her of the unaffected man who'd gotten dirt under his fingernails while working beside her. But his voice was warm and welcoming as she turned and stepped into his arms.

"God, I've missed you," he said, clutching her close, holding her so tightly she could barely breathe. She didn't care, though. When he held her like this, she felt wanted and secure. As always, his touch erased the doubts.

"It's only been four days," she murmured, then took advantage of the height her heels lent her and touched her lips to his before he could speak again. His lips were warm and responsive beneath hers. Then the tenor of the kiss changed. His hands slid slowly down her back and pressed her against him, letting her know exactly how much he'd missed her. And what he'd missed.

"We'd better go inside," Beth said. "The elevator . . . your neighbors . . ."

As Beth backed out of the embrace, Justin took her hand and pulled her inside, closing the door behind them. Then he halted. "I'm sorry. Your luggage. I forgot." He reached for the knob.

Beth had the grace to look sheepish. "I left it with the doorman. He thought I was with the group I walked in with. And I imagine they're all sitting around the eighth floor now, wondering who I am."

Justin chuckled. "I'd better ask Beatrice to call down before the doorman chucks everything out into the street."

Hearing her name, the older woman appeared.

"I guess I won't be needing this," she said, dangling the pistol from her fingertips.

Justin grinned down at Beth, still holding her. "Not this time, Beatrice. This is the lady I was supposed to pick up at the airport later. Some surprise, huh?"

"You said you weren't going to be here this weekend. Have you changed your mind, sir? I could cancel my plans," Beatrice offered. The words were respectful, but the tone matched her dour expression.

"No need. We'll be leaving after a bit," he explained, adding instructions about Beth's luggage.

"Leaving?" Beth asked. The whole point of this trip was for her to see where and how he lived, wasn't it?

"Yes, I'd planned on picking you up at the airport and going directly from there," he explained. "As it is, you've upset Beatrice's sense of order. She thought you were a reporter."

Beth's misgivings returned. He hadn't even planned for her to see his home. Was he hiding something or did he guess she wouldn't feel comfortable here? The cold marble tile from the foyer continued down the hall, butting up against several rooms with icy-white carpeting. All black and white and trimmed with chrome, Justin's apartment seemed foreign and unwelcoming.

He must have sensed the change in her, but he mistook the cause. "Don't let Beatrice bother you. She's naturally grumpy, but she's good at her job. And she keeps the nuts from bothering me."

"I think *she's* nuts," Beth whispered uneasily.

"Don't worry," Justin answered. "The gun isn't real. It's a plastic stage prop, left over from my college days. She uses it to scare off the occasional reporter or fan who follows me home and slips past the doorman downstairs."

"I suppose she's usually effective."

He dropped a quick kiss on Beth's nose. "You're her first failure."

"Did she threaten your other guests?" Beth asked, gesturing vaguely in the direction of his living room and the low buzz of conversation.

"Melanie let them in. She was tied up when you arrived or you wouldn't have had any of this trouble," he said. "In fact, if you'd called, I would have picked you up at the airport."

"I tried, but the line was busy," Beth said. "Finally I gave up and took a cab."

"I'm sorry," interrupted a clear, decisive voice. Justin's sister stepped into the hall, her heels clicking firmly against the tiles. "I was on the phone for hours. Business," she explained. "And some travel arrangements Justin asked me to make."

"Not another word," he said. "It's a surprise."

Melanie's dark brows lifted in surprise. "You mean you haven't told her about Gull House and—" Justin's hand clamped over her mouth before she could spill the secret, and he playfully threatened his sister with a mock blow to the nose.

"I'd like to be a fly on the wall," she said when he released her. "Are you coming in, or do you intend to sneak away without telling anyone? Don't forget I haven't even told you which airport yet or even what time the pilot—"

"Shut up, woman," he told his sister, while he led Beth toward the buzzing conversation.

Beth's eyes widened in surprise at the group assembled there. Two dozen people, near as she could tell, lounged or stood about the room. Several avidly curious pairs of eyes settled on her, and she automatically donned her social face, hiding her irritation beneath a composed expression.

"Come on. I'll get you a drink," Melanie said. "What would you like? Wine? Scotch? Or are you one of those health nuts who won't touch the stuff?"

Beth smiled. She wasn't, but alcohol loosened her tongue, such as when she'd first had dinner with Justin. "Juice if you have it. Or water. I don't want to embarrass myself in front of Justin's friends," she said in a light tone designed to turn the truth into a flip comment.

"Friends?" Melanie grimaced. "This is business, mostly people connected with 'Vice Cops.' Except for Tony, Justin's agent, and of course, Vincent," she added, indicating the sharp-chinned, balding man, one of a pair who'd joined them, and presented their glasses for refills. Justin complied with the easy familiarity of an old friend.

The older one looked vaguely familiar, but Beth was sure she'd never met the man. She had no doubt about the identity of the other man the moment he spoke, having taken several calls from him when Justin wasn't available.

"I heard my name. What about me?" Tony asked. His manner was as smooth and calculating as the careful part in his neatly combed hair and the unmarred shine of his shoes.

Melanie smiled. "Relax, Tony, or I'll scuff your shoes."

"Beth, meet Vincent Underwood," Justin said, introducing her to the remaining stranger. "He's the producer of 'Vice Cops.' And he's the poor guy who Tony conned into backing *Nebraska Sky*. Vincent, this is Beth Thompson."

"Just the woman I've been looking for," Vincent said, offering Beth his outstretched hand. She smiled, and grasped his hand firmly, remembering not to gouge him with the unfamiliar length of the glued-on fingernails she wore to cover her own chipped and work-stained ones. Beth couldn't imagine what the man would have to talk to her about, but she hid her thoughts and waited for him to explain.

"The location manager has hit a snag," Vincent continued. "The owner of the farm where we'd planned to shoot most of the outdoor scenes died before he signed the contract. His family isn't too interested and they've been stalling. Justin mentioned earlier that your place might work."

"Beth grows vegetables. It's a produce operation, not a wheat farm," Justin said.

Vincent looked to Beth for confirmation, frowning when she agreed. "Couldn't you replant?" he suggested. "How long does wheat take to come up? We aren't scheduled to start filming for a few weeks yet.

We could begin with the shots up by the house and barn, leave the field shots until the wheat's ready.''

"It wouldn't work," Justin hesitated. "The hills are too big. It wouldn't look right. No one who's seen Nebraska would believe it."

Vincent shrugged. "If you say so. Having never been to Missouri or Nebraska, I'll just have to take your word for it."

From there the conversation drifted on to a particularly colorful state politician who'd been caught with his hand in the till. Beth was actually beginning to enjoy herself when a set of red-nailed talons curled over Justin's arm. An unexpected wave of jealousy surged through her, stiffening her spine and straining her smile.

"Justin dear," the blonde cooed, in a voice that eerily reminded Beth of Marlene. "Steve is on the phone. He wants us all to come back in tomorrow for another take on the bar scene. Maybe you can talk him out of it." Beth remembered Justin telling her about Steve Lund, the exacting director of the hit show.

Justin nodded as he uncurled the fingers from his arm and dropped a kiss on Beth's nose. "Be right back," he said, then directed his attention to the blonde. "I'll take it in the kitchen. Hang up out here when I pick up the extension."

The look the blonde shot Beth was murderous, but Beth was more shaken by her own reaction than any potential threat from that woman.

"Smooth," Melanie whispered. "That puts him in the kitchen with Beatrice, safely away from Cassandra's roving fingers."

Still watching the pouting blonde, who'd sidled up

to Tony, Beth nodded and whispered back. "She seems predatory."

Melanie shrugged. "Some like the type," she said. "Come on, I'll introduce you around."

Sometime later, Beth scanned the room for the umpteenth time, looking for Justin. More than half an hour ago, Melanie had abandoned her to the company of a gaffer, two stuntmen, and one of Justin's co-stars. They had recounted various mishaps on the set until tears of laughter streamed from her eyes. Then gradually they'd drifted away, one by one, until only the gaffer was left, and he'd fallen asleep on the couch beside her.

She checked the kitchen first, then what looked to be the study before the low murmur of voices drew her toward a third doorway. Justin's bedroom was like the rest of the house, stark black and white, with only a small clutter of items at one end of the dresser to identify who lived there—spare change, loosely scattered snapshots, and a newspaper clipping of Beth's windblown skirt that first night in Kansas City.

But it was the voices drifting in from the terrace that stopped her in her tracks.

"Don't you think you should let Beth make up her own mind about Vincent's offer?" Melanie was saying. Justin mumbled something in response, but Beth couldn't make out the words. So she stepped closer, standing in the darkness next to the fluttering white curtain that covered the wide, sliding door to the terrace.

"But if she needs money—" Melanie argued.

"She's not broke. She just has to be careful, that's all," Justin answered. "Like Mom and Dad when we were kids. The farm seems to be turning a profit, but it could use a bit of work, new fences, repairs, paint."

"All the more reason for filming there," Melanie argued. "You know Vincent. He'd order the place painted and the grounds manicured before the cameras were unpacked. It'd save her the trouble and the expense."

Beth leaned back against the wall waiting in the long silence for his answer, thinking how the farm must look through his eyes. He wouldn't imagine the neat, new fence Grandma and Charley had built, with the dubious help of a half-wild, barefoot girl. He'd only see the sagging, rusted wire and leaning fenceposts that were there now. And the Bridal's Veil bushes that half covered the windows would only be overgrown shrubbery to trim back or cut down altogether.

But his words, when he finally spoke, surprised her.

"They'd ruin the place," he said. "It'd be like taking the magic out of Oz."

Melanie's confused laugh cut through Beth's amazement. "Magic?"

"Well, not magic, exactly. But there's something special about the place, something timeless, about all those generations of people who lived there and raised children in that house. And the barn—did you know it was built with square nails and wooden pegs? It must have taken ten men to wedge those huge beams together."

"There's nothing magic about square nails. So the place is old. It sounds like the kind of atmosphere Vincent's trying to capture in this film."

"It has atmosphere, all right," Justin continued. "Vincent's crew would change it into something Beth wouldn't recognize. And there'd be people everywhere once word got out—not just the crew and the cast, but the press and fans and half the state."

"It sounds to me, Big Brother, like you want to keep your little hideaway a secret. And don't give me that look. You like it there. Otherwise Tony wouldn't have had so much trouble dragging you back."

"I wish I was there now," he said in a voice that was both wistful and full of warmth. "It feels more like home than this place."

Melanie laughed. "You should redecorate."

"Why bother? I'm thinking of selling it."

"That might be easier."

Beth heard the soft creak of someone settling into a deck chair. "It's not the carpeting or the wallpaper," Justin confided. "It's deeper than that. I'm tired of living this way. I have been for a long time."

Melanie's sigh was barely audible. "Don't get any ideas about turning farmer. You have a contract with Vincent's company. You can't afford to break it," she reminded him. "Besides, you no more belong on a farm than I do. It's too mundane, too boring. You're just infatuated. Get it out of your system before you do something stupid like marry her. She's nice, but she's not your type."

"Don't go bitter on me, Mel, just because your marriage turned out to be a mess," Justin warned.

"Sorry. I guess you're old enough to make your own mistakes."

"It wouldn't be a mistake," Justin said. "I love her."

"Oh, please," Melanie said in an exasperated tone. "Where have I heard that before? I told Mom and Dad something like that before I married David. Look where it got me. But I don't expect you to listen to me, not in your condition. So I'll just give you the flight schedule and let you and Beth be on your way."

Before she could reach the door, Beth had slipped quietly from the room and leaned against the hallway wall, considering what she'd just heard. After seeing his apartment, seeing him with these people, she understood why he felt dissatisfied. This place was cold and soulless. Not like home. And he felt it, too. She was beginning to believe it could work between them, that somehow they could find a way to make it work.

TEN

Beth awoke the next morning with a sense of well-being and a soft, satisfied smile on her lips. Although judging from the high angle of the sun, the morning was pretty much past. She was alone in the big bed. But the twisted, rumpled covers and the indentation on the other pillow reminded her that she hadn't been that way all night.

She blushed even lying there alone when she remembered the night before, the heated kiss in the back of the taxi that took them to the airport. A chartered plane had carried them from L.A. to the Monterey Peninsula Airport, where Justin had claimed yet another of his cars. Then he'd driven her here to this strange house on the beach and made magnificent love to her. Pale streaks of dawn had lit the sky before they slept.

She wrapped the blue-striped sheet around her and stepped lightly to the window. Justin sat on the top step of the deck that rose above the sand at the back of the house, reading from a bound stack of typed sheets, but he looked up when Beth opened the window.

"Good morning," he called.

She shivered a little as the chill ocean wind brushed her bare shoulders. "I thought it was hot in California," she replied. "This feels like October."

"Around here, it never gets hot, something about the cool ocean currents," he said. "Nice, isn't it?"

Beth smiled. "Actually it is, kind of like a crisp fall morning. What's for breakfast? Or should I say lunch?"

"Canned peas or Tuna Helper without the tuna unless we go shopping," he answered.

"I vote for shopping. I'll be down in a minute," she called, then went in search of her suitcase.

She found it at the foot of the bed and quickly slipped on a new pair of jeans and a light cotton blouse, the warmest clothing she'd brought. Then she stepped barefoot down the hallway to explore this strange house. It perched on a point of rock overlooking the sea at the end of a bumpy, little-traveled road. It was old, she knew, built before any outcry about saving the seashores from development.

By moonlight the house had risen eerily from the sand, looking like the perfect home for a discontented ghost. The shingled roof looked like it had shifted and buckled through the years—the clever trick of construction that made the cottage appear centuries old and brimming with atmosphere and whimsy. Its strange roofline, the stone chimney and the shingle siding reminded Beth of a fairy tale cottage, or maybe the witch's house in Hansel and Gretel.

The interior had obviously been renovated recently. It was all airiness and open space, not boxy and cluttered as the outside had led her to believe. The scattering of comfortable, modern furnishings also seemed incongruous in the quaint, storybook house.

"Why do you call this Gull House?" she asked Justin as she joined him on the back deck. "The name doesn't seem to fit."

He set the script aside and tugged her down into his lap. "I don't want to talk about the house. I want to kiss you."

"Didn't you get enough of that last night?" she teased, even as she snuggled close, soaking up his warmth. She lifted her lips for his kiss and let the familiar wave of pleasure flow over her.

"That's better," he murmured when he lifted his head.

"Mmm. You didn't answer my question," she said.

"First a little nourishment, then we'll see about picking up where we left off last night."

"This morning," she corrected him. "But that's the wrong question. I want to know where this place got its name. I don't see any gulls."

"They're around, sometimes flocks of them out there along the beach. I got the feeling when I first came here that the locals would be offended if I renamed the house. I'd just as soon keep them happy since they watch over the place when I'm gone and keep my presence a secret when I'm here."

"Do you own the house?"

He nodded. "I bought it a couple of years ago, during the hiatus after shooting the first year of 'Vice Cops'. At first it was just a place to get away to. Now it's home. L.A.'s just a place I go to."

"That's understandable," she answered. "This is comfortable. Strange, but comfortable. That apartment of yours is—"

"Horrible," he finished. "Tony found it for me. He thought it fit the image, and I guess it does. It's perfect for entertaining reporters, letting them see what they think is the real me. I like it here better. Mel and I both come here every chance we get. What do you think of it?''

She glanced around, her eyes settling on the barren yard that was mostly sand with a few scrubby, unfamiliar weeds scattered about. She was surprised anything could grow there. ''It's interesting. A bit dry and barren, but a nice vacation spot, I guess. What's this you're reading?'' she asked, picking up the thickly bound stack.

''Nothing important. Just a script,'' he said, taking it from her before she could find the title. ''Let's go find some food.''

''Fine, just let me call Aunt Eva first and leave her this number in case she needs to reach me.''

''Give her and Charley my best,'' he called. ''I'll wait out front.''

Aunt Eva answered on the third ring, sounding flustered and excited. ''Beth dear, how is Los Angeles?''

''Different, but that's not where I am,'' Beth said, gazing out the window at the sand. Briefly, she explained about Gull House, then asked after Charley and the farm's operations.

''Everything's fine. And the man from the lumberyard delivered the supplies late Friday. The boys replaced some of those old posts near the barn, and they're working in the north pasture now.''

''I didn't order any supplies.''

''Your name was on the ticket. I saw it when I signed for the delivery.''

''It's a mistake,'' Beth insisted. ''I made a list up, but I didn't plan to get anything until after I sell the corn.''

"Oh, dear," Aunt Eva murmured. "You didn't give it to Charley, did you? Maybe he misunderstood."

"No. It was on my desk in the office. He wouldn't just take it upon himself to order them, would he?"

Aunt Eva sighed. "I don't know. What should I do?"

"How much was the bill?" Beth winced at the amount, then ordered the work stopped and the unused materials returned. There was no way she could cover the full amount now.

"I just hope the lumberyard will accept them," Aunt Eva said before hanging up.

"Something wrong?" Justin asked when Beth climbed into the car.

"Just a mix-up," she said with a crooked smile. "The lumberyard delivered some supplies I didn't order. Aunt Eva's straightening it out."

Justin tried to look concerned, but a glitter in his eyes destroyed the effect. "What kind of supplies?"

"Fenceposts. Wire."

His grin widened. "Maybe you should keep it. It wouldn't go to waste."

"I can't pay for it, not yet. You know that."

He hesitated, as if about to argue. Then he simply shrugged and let the subject drop. Instead, he quizzed her on what she wanted for breakfast and where they should eat. After much debate, they settled on an early lunch in a quiet, out-of-the-way restaurant run by a Mexican family. Then they spent the afternoon on the scenic seventeen-mile drive through the Pebble Beach and Del Monte Forest area.

After that, they amused themselves by driving the residential streets of Carmel, gawking like tourists at the houses. The sometimes quaint, often unique architectural styles were visual reminders that this city began as an artists' colony. She wished she'd brought her plant encyclopedia so she could identify the tall clusters of blue flowers that bloomed so abundantly. Then something else caught her eye.

"Stop," Beth ordered excitedly, leaning out the window to view a house that looked much like Justin's. "I can't believe it. Who would have thought there could be two? They've copied your house." The chimney was on the opposite side, but otherwise this house was architecturally the same. However, the crooked stile fence and artfully arranged shrubs and plants complemented the house in a way the bare sand and washed-up kelp at Gull House never would.

"Mine's the copy, according to the real-estate agent I used," Justin explained as he eased the car onto the shoulder of the narrow street to allow traffic behind him to pass. "But it caught my imagination. And it has privacy." He made privacy sound as important as electricity and indoor plumbing.

She knew how precious privacy was to him. Hadn't he rejected Vincent's proposal for that reason, because Thompson Farm would no longer be a refuge for him if it were opened up to the film crew and hordes of lookers-on. He hadn't said that in so many words, but Beth had picked up the underlying thread to his argument.

She was ready for that privacy herself after a hectic hour in the grocery store, ducking the attentions of the curious and sometimes overly bold shoppers who recognized Justin. No one had been rude, but it was disconcerting to be the focus of so much attention.

"Does this always happen?" she asked when they were once again on their way.

"Usually Mel does the shopping. Or we have the groceries delivered."

"I don't blame you. I felt like a prize fish in a pet shop. How come nobody noticed us in the restaurant or when we were driving around?"

"Dim lighting. Tinted windows."

"No crowds," Beth added. "The restaurant was practically deserted, and you hid under a hat and sunglasses whenever we got out of the car this afternoon."

"Now you know," he said. "Maybe I'll grow back the beard, just until I start filming."

She shook her head. "You'll give your makeup artist fits with that uneven tan line," she answered. After that, they rounded a curve and the sight of the sand, rocks, and gnarled cypress trees chased away the tension of the last hour.

They kept to themselves that evening and all of the next day, walking along the beach and wetting their feet in the chill waters. Dinner was a quiet picnic in front of the fireplace, with the phone deliberately left off the cradle. And when they left their warm bed for a midnight snack, they wore only bedsheets, loosely wrapped with a tendency for slipping.

The next day, they fed the Beechey Ground squirrels that lived among the rocks nearby and watched the sandpipers run on toothpick legs to escape the surf. They raced in the sand, with dinner as the prize, then compromised on the terms of defeat—Justin cooked and Beth cleaned up.

She had just drained the dishwater from the sink when she noticed how quiet the house had become. Thinking Justin had gone outside, she slipped out the back door onto the deck. But his sand-encrusted sneakers were still on the step. Then she noticed the curtain fluttering in the open bedroom window on the second floor. She'd closed that same window less than an hour ago, when she'd come out of the shower.

"Incorrigible," she said, grinning as she slipped back through the door. She thought of how she'd surprised him the night before, wearing nothing but a silk-and-lacy teddy that was mostly lace. And the pink garters.

She tiptoed up the stairs, growing warmer with each step just from her thoughts. When she peeked through the half-open door, she was surprised to find Justin seated in the deep pile chair near the window, reading from the stack of typed pages again.

He looked up and smiled when one of the polished floorboards creaked beneath her feet.

"I'll read this later," he said.

"Don't you have that memorized by now?" she asked, indicating what looked to be the *Nebraska* script.

"This is a new one," he explained. "Vincent gave it to me last week, but I didn't have a chance to look at it until we got up here." He watched her carefully, as if afraid of her reaction.

She didn't know what to think, so she kept her expression neutral.

"What's it about?"

He shrugged. "Another adventure flick. Not exactly inspired material. But with Vincent's magic touch, it could be a blockbuster hit."

"You don't seem too excited about that."

"Tony thinks it's a good career move. I'm not so sure. I want to break out of the mold, not dig myself in deeper."

"So don't take the part."

"I already have. That's part of the deal I made with Vincent on *Nebraska Sunset*."

She nodded, not pleased with the knowledge, but not willing to let it spoil their weekend. "In that case, you'd better read it."

"There's no rush," he offered, but already his eyes were fastened on the page.

"I should check in with Charley and Aunt Eva anyway," she said, smiling sadly as he grunted in response and turned a page. Already, he was slipping away from her, she thought, as she headed downstairs to use the kitchen phone. He might deny it, but he loved his work, even the macho flicks.

She mentally calculated the time difference and decided Charley and Aunt Eva would probably be at the house by now getting ready for dinner. But when Charley answered, she could hear the rattle of tools and casual banter between the teenagers who worked for her.

"Are you working in the shed? And what are the boys doing there on a Sunday?" she asked, frowning into the receiver. He ought to be resting, not putting in extra hours while she was gone.

"Just finishin' up," Charley answered, sounding tired. "Didn't realize how late it was gettin' till Eva came down to the field where we were workin' and chewed me out good."

"Somebody should," Beth retorted.

"I ain't no invalid," the old man grumbled. "You women act like I got one foot in the grave."

"Never mind that," she said. "Did Aunt Eva call the lumberyard?"

"What in tarnation for? And what's this nonsense about stopping work on the fence? Me and the boys are nearly finished with the north pasture. Fixed that old black Witch up real good. She won't be able to get out that new gate, either."

"What gate? Charley! I can't pay for that stuff now."

"It's already paid for. It's written right on the receipt. Eva called to double-check, and you don't owe a dime. Got a twenty-dollar credit, in fact, 'cause old Hal added wrong when Justin placed the order."

Beth clenched the receiver tightly. "Justin placed the order?" she repeated. Suddenly it made sense.

"He signed the ticket. Paid by check, they said, and Eva's hoppin' mad 'cause you didn't write it down before you left. Said she can't make the books balance when you do that and—"

"Never mind, Charley," she interrupted, then slammed the receiver onto the cradle without so much as a good-bye.

She took the stairs two at a time and stormed into the bedroom, startling Justin.

"You have a hell of a nerve," she shouted as she cleared the doorway. "Thompson Farm is mine. I decide when to buy new fenceposts and when to paint the barn. And when I do, I write the check." As she spoke, she advanced closer until she leaned over him, punctuating each word with her pointed finger.

Justin leaned back and sighed resignedly. "You found out."

"Of course I did! Did you think I wouldn't notice that the fence didn't sag anymore or that the barn was another color when I got back home?"

He at least had the grace to wince. "I thought I'd be there when the stuff arrived. I guess they brought it early."

"That's not the point," she said. "It's my responsibility, my profit or loss. I don't need anybody going behind my back and second-guessing me. When I can afford to buy paint, I'll buy paint."

Then he frowned. "I didn't order any paint."

"Well, why not? You ordered damn near everything else on my list."

"I didn't know what color to get."

She threw up her hands in exasperation. "I'm going for a walk. Alone," she added when he started to rise from the chair.

She whirled and stomped out of the house, ignoring his footsteps behind her until he called her name in a tone that stopped her in her tracks.

"I'm sorry," he said. When she didn't answer, he sagged against the doorjamb. "Where are you going?" he asked.

"I don't know. I need to think."

"Stay out of the water," he called as she turned back toward the beach. "There's a pretty strong undertow."

She cast an incredulous look over her shoulder. "Yes, Mother," she called and stalked on, cursing the sand that turned her dignified escape into sliding lurches.

She didn't know how far she walked, following the shoreline. The arguments chasing back in forth in her mind erased all sense of time. Maybe she was too sensitive about anything remotely disguised as a threat to her independence. But damn it, he'd gone too far. She wouldn't have dared manipulate him that way. But he hadn't intended it that way, had he? Wasn't he only trying to help, to relieve some of the financial burden weighing her down? It was a piddling amount of money to him, but it was a lot to her, and therein lay their differences.

It wasn't until she noticed the deepening angle of the sun that she turned back, still not sure what to do. She knew what she should do. She should leave and not look back, walk away while she still could. If she still could.

She found Justin at sunset, sitting in the sand a short distance from Gull House.

"I was worried," he told her.

She settled into the cool sand beside him, close enough to touch but not touching.

"I can take care of myself."

"I know that," he said. "I also know that you were upset and distracted. And it was my fault."

"That's just it," she said softly, as the understanding that had eluded her slipped into place. "You're starting to feel responsible for me. You shouldn't, you know."

The silence stretched between them until she thought, sadly, that he hadn't anything to say, that he didn't understand. But before she could bring herself to explain something she wasn't sure she could put into words, he shifted and took her hand.

"I'm sorry. I didn't mean to step on your toes. I knew you might argue, but I thought I could make you see the sense in it. You were going to buy those things in the fall anyway, but you need them now. What good is a new fence in the fall if the cattle disappeared in the summer?"

She smiled and shook her head at the same time. The man didn't give up. He could apologize and justify himself in the same breath and still sound sincere.

"You're right about the fences," she admitted. "But that's not the issue."

"No, the issue is this misplaced sense of independence you have," he said. "There's a difference between independence and outright stubbornness."

"I'm not stubborn," she retorted, trying to pull her hand away, then gave up. "Okay," she admitted after a bit. "Maybe I'm stubborn. But I have to be. Sometimes that's all that keeps me going."

"Asking for help isn't a failure."

"No. But there's a difference between accepting help and becoming dependent. I'm starting to depend too much on you, and that's not good for either of us."

"You depend on your aunt to help with the paperwork. Not too long ago, you left it all to her," he pointed out.

"That's different and you know it," she said.

"So consider this a loan. Pay me back at harvest."

"What if the crop fails? Or if the yield is low and I don't make enough on it to cover the planting loan?"

"It can wait."

She shook her head. "The bank wouldn't let me wait. Not with my outstanding loans."

"I'm not going to convince you, am I?"

A half-smile crossed her lips. "I'm stubborn, remember."

"I didn't think the money would matter," he said. "It's not that important to me."

"Money is always important."

"I was going to ask you to marry me. Tonight. In bed. After we made love."

Beth didn't know whether to laugh or cry. She leaned against him, laying her head against his shoulder.

"Oh, Justin," she whispered. "What am I going to do about you?"

"Love me," he replied. "Marry me."

She forced herself upright again. "I wish I could."

"I suppose you have a good reason?" He dropped her hand and stood, his back to her, fists on his hips.

"I just know it wouldn't work. I'll hate it when I don't see you anymore, but I'll survive. If I keep depending on you—for money, for answers, just for smiles—then you'll be too much a part of me. I don't think I could survive if you left then."

"Why are you so damned sure I'll leave? Do you really think so little of yourself? Or is it me you don't trust?"

"You're way off track," she retorted. "I'm a challenge. Someone new and different. Someone that happened to you when you were between projects. When you get caught up in your work again, you'll only have bits and pieces of time for me. I'll resent that and we'll end up tearing at each other. And if there were children, well, what we'd do to them doesn't bear thinking about."

"Other actors manage. I know two who bring their families with them when they're filming. Another actress has a nursery next to her dressing room on the set."

"I couldn't live that way," she said. "I need roots and I have them now. If I give all that up, I'll lose everything I've tried to accomplish. I'll end up like Marlene. Dependent. Nothing of her own, not even inside. I won't let it happen."

"Why does it have to be all or nothing with you? Why can't you compromise?"

"Because sometimes there isn't one that will work," she insisted.

"Then I guess we're at an impasse," he said in a

tight, chilled tone. "You can't compromise, and I can't keep fighting you."

She stood and reached out to him, touching his hand until he turned. "It's been good, hasn't it?" she whispered.

"Best two months of my life," he answered, his voice cracking. He pulled her close, and they clung together as the sun dipped below the horizon.

They made love that night with slow, reverent touches and a deep savoring that brought Beth to peaks she'd never imagined. They made love as if they both knew it had to last forever, as if it were the last time.

It was, Beth thought as they lay together in the cool dawn, he asleep and she staring at the ceiling, putting off the moment when she would leave the warmth of his bed. She'd thought it through. She'd spent the whole night thinking while Justin had slept. He'd deceived her, but with the best of intentions. Still, their differences were too great. He'd always want to do more for her, to provide now what she was willing to save for, whether it took months or years to accumulate enough money. And in doing so, he'd rob her of the pride and self-confidence of such hard-won accomplishments. He'd unwittingly steal her self-respect. Better to end it now than to let those differences slowly eat at them until there was nothing good left to remember.

When the mantel clock chimed downstairs, Beth tensed. She knew she could wait no longer. Slowly, so she wouldn't wake Justin, she moved the arm that was draped across her midsection and slid her leg from beneath his. She dressed quickly, and hurried downstairs to call a taxi.

She tried three companies before she found one willing to come out so far at that hour. Relieved, she gave the dispatcher her name and directions to the house.

"Is that the old Tanney place, the one with the turrets?" the woman asked.

"No," Beth answered. "It's called Gull House."

"Sure," the woman snorted. "Do you know how many Gull Houses there are out that way."

"Justin said all the locals know it by that name." Then she repeated the directions, mentally reviewing the drive. "The name on the mailbox is Schnell," she added.

While she waited, she slipped back upstairs and quietly packed her small bag. As she retrieved her nightgown from beneath the bed, Justin stirred. She sat up and held her breath until he rolled over and wrapped his arm around her pillow before releasing a loud, snorting snore.

The sound brought a fleeting smile to her lips. She leaned over and lightly kissed his brow, then backed slowly out of the room. The next ten minutes seemed an eternity, but when the taxi pulled in front of the house and honked, she perversely wished the driver had taken longer. Her hand hesitated on the doorknob as she glanced back at the stairs. But all was silent on the floor above her.

Then her eyes fell on the script, lying on a side table, and her indecision vanished. She stepped onto the porch, closing the door behind her.

"You the lady who called for a taxi?" the driver called as he walked up the sidewalk.

"That's me. I just have the one bag," she said, handing it over to him. He had just stowed it in the trunk when the front door whipped open and Justin stormed out. Bare to the waist, he clutched a wrinkled towel around his hips.

"What are you doing?" he bellowed.

"Going home," Beth replied, keeping her voice level, although her hands trembled so badly she could barely work the latch.

"Your flight isn't until this afternoon," he pointed out, striding closer and tugging at the slipping towel at the same time.

"I'll catch an earlier one. If there isn't one, I'll just find something to read while I wait."

He reached out with his free hand and grabbed her arm before she could climb inside the car. He'd awakened to the sound of a car horn, and thought he was only dreaming until he realized that he was hugging a cold, lifeless pillow instead of the passionate woman he'd made love to half the night.

"You were just going to sneak away without saying good-bye, without an explanation," he said. "Why?"

"Good grief. Sneak?" she retorted. "You're the last one who should talk about sneaking around after what you did."

"You're still angry about the fenceposts? I apologized. What more do you want? I thought you understood why I did it."

"I do understand. But that doesn't change anything."

The hell it didn't, Justin thought. Last night he'd sensed an opening, a window of indecision, and he'd attacked that window with everything he had. And when she'd come to him, when she'd cried out in ecstasy in his arms, he thought she'd realized how perfect they were together, how completely he loved her.

Justin drew a deep breath, then spoke in a low, throaty voice that tugged at her soul. "You made love to me like you really meant it, like it was a promise. Were you just pretending?''

Beth forced herself to look beyond him to the house. ''I love you. But it's not enough. Last night didn't change anything,'' she insisted, shaking her head slowly.

''What was it then? An act? No. I get it. It all makes sense now,'' he said as comprehension dawned in his expression, followed immediately by a cynical smirk. ''You planned this all along, you and that crazy mother of yours. You played the sincere, country innocent so I wouldn't suspect you were out for big game. Well what happened? Did you chicken out? Is that why you're leaving? Or don't I have enough money after all?''

Beth paled. ''Look, I didn't want it to be like this. That's why I didn't wake you. I just have to leave. You know my reasons, the real reasons, not this junk you dreamed up.'' Beth threw a sidelong glance at the wide-eyed taxi driver.

''Don't mind me,'' he said with an interested nod. ''I'll just smoke a cigarette and you let me know when you're ready to go.''

''Now,'' Beth ground out.

''No,'' Justin argued, tugging her away from the car. ''If you want to leave, I'll drive you to the airport. Now pay the man for his trouble, and let's go back inside. This towel is damn drafty.''

Neither of them noticed the arrival of a second car until it was too late. The vehicle had barely rolled to a stop when the whirring click of a camera and an electronic flash of light drew their attention.

''Oh, my God!'' Beth whispered as Bob Greeno advanced on them. To her dying day, she'd remember the smirk on the sleazy tabloid reporter's stubby face. She turned back to Justin. "How did he find us?"

But Justin's expression was colder than polished marble. "The taxi," he replied. "He's probably bribed half the dispatchers in town. These people make a lot of money stalking celebrities."

"I didn't think . . ." Beth began.

"You're damn right, you didn't think. How could you have been so stupid as to call a public taxi and give directions to my house? Hell, you probably gave my name, too. You practically handed the creep an engraved invitation," Justin berated in a low voice. "Or maybe you called him yourself."

"What? Oh, I suppose that fits right in with this gold-digger theory of yours."

"Yeah. It does. Now get into the house before this gets any worse."

Beth felt herself flush and she backed away. "No," she replied. "There's nothing left to say. I'll have someone send your things."

"If that's the way you want it, fine," he retorted angrily, then he turned to Greeno. "And you get off my property before I have you arrested for trespassing and harassment."

"Just leaving," Greeno replied. "I have all I need anyway. By the way, nice legs." He slammed the door closed and jerked the still-running car into gear and sped down the driveway, leaving a thick cloud of dust whirling among the fading fog.

Beth's eyes sought Justin's, and she shook her head pleadingly. "I'm sorry," she said. "I didn't want it to be this way. I thought it'd be easier on us both if I left quietly."

The steely glint in his eyes sent shivers down her

spine. "I'd like to believe you mean that," he said. "But right now, I'm finding it hard just looking at you." The words were a lash on her already battered heart, and Beth squeezed her eyes closed. She didn't open them again until she heard the front door slam closed.

Then she climbed into the taxi and let the tears stream down her face, heedless of the driver's pitying glance in the mirror. All she could see was Justin's cold, disappointed expression, and it was like a knife twisting in her chest. He hadn't meant what he said about the money, she knew that. He was just angry. But he was right about one thing—she'd managed to destroy the one refuge he had. Gull House was no longer a secret. And she doubted he'd ever forgive her for that.

With an effort, she regained control of herself and told the driver to take her to the airport. The rest of the trip passed in a blur of misery, but by the time the plane touched down at Kansas City International Airport, she'd recovered her composure. She was able to greet Charley and Aunt Eva with a smile and a hug. And if they noticed the shallowness of her happiness, they kept it to themselves.

ELEVEN

"Come on, Beth," Charley wheedled. "One game. I'll even lend you some bottlecaps—"

"Leave her alone, you old fool," Aunt Eva interjected. "If she doesn't feel like playing, she doesn't feel like it."

"It's a fine state when a man can't even get up an innocent card game after supper," the old man grumbled. "Now, that Justin was a good sport. You never did tell us, girl, why he never came back?"

Beth simply ignored him, just as she had for most of the month since she'd returned from California. She'd come to terms with the situation, but she couldn't shake the leaden feeling in her heart. That would take a bit more time.

"Why don't you call the boy?" Charley suggested.

Aunt Eva released a long-suffering sigh. "I'll play with you," she said. "But only if you'll shut up and mind your own business."

Despite her annoyance, Beth almost smiled at the sparkle that lit Charley's rheumy eyes.

"Well, now, might I take that as a sign that you've decided to be willin'?" Charley asked.

"Maybe," Aunt Eva replied, her face flushing as she fumbled with the cards. "What do you think, old man?"

"I think you're toyin' with my affections," he replied as he slapped a deck onto the side table that stood between their chairs. "Then again, you never offered to play before, never thought you knew how. Does this mean you've decided something I might need to know about?"

"It means that I'm tired of listenin' to you grumble and I've decided to shut you up."

"You gonna marry me or not?"

"Yes."

The two of them glared at each other over the table like professional boxers entering the ring.

"Saturday," Charley barked.

"Done."

A broad grin split Charley's wrinkled face. "Wear your blue dress. You look pretty in it."

Aunt Eva's jaw worked, but no sound came out.

The shrill jangle of the phone split the temporary silence. Beth rose to get it, moving distractedly into the hall. She snatched up the receiver and dashed back to the corner, dragging the phone after her. The tightness in her chest moved up to her throat as she watched two sets of wrinkled, work-worn hands clasp across the table. Then the indignant voice in her ear claimed her attention.

"Hello? Hello? Is this Thompson Farm?"

"Marlene!" Beth answered, her voice husky with emotion.

"Beth, is that you? I thought it was some heavy

breather, but wouldn't that be the oddest thing, a backward obscene phone call?'' Marlene rambled on. "Anyway, I just called to talk some sense into you.''

Beth closed her eyes, praying for strength and tact. "Mind your own business, Mother," she said.

"Oh, dear. You must really be upset. What exactly happened? Aunt Eva's letter didn't say. I thought you caught the man. He didn't have a wife stashed in California, did he? Because if he did, I'm going to report this to the auction committee.''

"Enough, Marlene. Did Aunt Eva tell you I passed the test? The results came in the mail last week. I'll finally have a diploma," she said, changing the subject.

"That's wonderful, dear," Marlene exclaimed. "That's one problem solved. Now about this little tiff you had with Justin—''

"It wasn't a little tiff, Mother. It just didn't work out. End of story.''

"Perhaps I should come home," she offered. "Sometimes it's easier to talk face-to-face.''

"No, there's no need. There's nothing to talk about." Somehow, she couldn't picture Marlene in the role of confidante.

"Honey, I know how it feels to be rejected, and—''

"It wouldn't have worked, Mother.''

"You could have taken a little time to think about it, at least. He could give you a good life, a lot better one than you have now. I'll bet you could even get him to pop the question if you played your cards right.''

"I like my life the way it is.''

Marlene's exaggerated sigh only irritated her daughter more. "Sometimes, Beth," Marlene wailed. "I think they made a mistake at the hospital and gave me the wrong baby. Why did you do such a fool thing?''

"I think it was the smart thing," Beth insisted, refusing to confess the doubts she'd harbored since the moment she'd stepped onto the plane home. She should have at least stayed long enough to convince Justin he'd jumped to the wrong conclusion, that she wasn't using him, just protecting herself.

"You know me," she said aloud. "I don't like crowds and socializing. I hate to be the center of attention, and believe me, that's what happens when you go out with Justin Kyle."

"That's a feeble excuse," Marlene retorted.

"I can't live that way. Besides, he's interfering with the farm. He'd take over if I let him, and I can't allow that. I won't give up my independence."

"Aunt Eva said something like that when she was about your age, from what I heard. Now look at her."

Beth did just that, then drew back, figuring some things should remain private. Like the kiss she'd just witnessed between the two most aggravating and precious people in her life. Happy as she was for them, she suddenly felt excluded from an important circle. The dull pain in her heart sharpened, and her eyes stung.

"I have a surprise for you, Marlene," Beth said, her voice low and soft with envy.

"You're not pregnant, are you?"

"Absolutely not. I'm not a fool."

Marlene's silence spoke louder than anything she could have said. "Well, what's the surprise?" she finally asked.

"Charley and Aunt Eva are getting married on Saturday."

"What? No, don't be ridiculous."

"You know I wouldn't lie about something like

that. They've been talking about it since Charley's accident.''

"I never would have thought it. That'll bring a few changes to the home place,'' Marlene said.

Beth was silent for a moment. "Sometimes changes are good,'' she finally said.

"Well, you should take a lesson from your aunt. She's a smart woman. Take your opportunities while you can,'' Marlene replied, agilely shifting her argument. "Like me and Alfred.''

"Be honest for once,'' Beth insisted. "You married Alfred because he's rich.''

"What an awful thing to say,'' Marlene said, sounding truly indignant. "That's not at all how it happened. I love Alfred very much. He's the most special, most wonderful man I know, and he treats me like a precious flower.''

"You never would have noticed him if he wasn't rich.''

"Of course not, dear. And that's just the point.''

"What?'' Beth asked. "Sorry, you lost me there.''

"You make your own luck in this world,'' Marlene declared. "I was tired of waiting tables and dodging passes from truck drivers. I wanted to live a better life, but the only way I knew was to find a rich man.''

"Isn't that what I said?''

"No. I may have dated for money, seeing only the ones who had good prospects, so to speak. But I married for love. There is a difference,'' Marlene explained in a hurt voice.

Beth scratched her temple as she plowed through Marlene's logic. "You really love Alfred?''

"Well, I suppose a child could get confused about

something like that. But you're a grown woman now. How could you ever think otherwise?"

But Beth had. All the signs had been there from the beginning—the tenderness in Marlene's voice, the frequent touches, the hundred small things the woman did to please Alfred. As a disillusioned, lonely teenager, she'd placed a different interpretation on them. But she should have known better, even then. She couldn't doubt the sincerity and pain in her mother's voice now. Beth felt terrible. And incredibly stupid. She'd let a false assumption influence her and thrown away the man she loved because of it.

"I'm sorry, Mother. All this time, I thought—"

"You should be," Marlene interrupted. "But it only proves what I always said. You remember, don't you? And I did fall in love with him."

"It's not always that simple. Sometimes . . ." Beth began, then jerked at the sharp thump on the wall behind her. "What the heck? Marlene, I have to go." Beth dropped the receiver before her mother could protest and hurried around the corner.

Charley banged his cane against the wall once more before he saw her. "There you are, girl. There's somebody here. Seems like you could take care of whatever it is they want since we're a bit occupied just now. What do you think? A church wedding or the courthouse?"

She glanced at her aunt.

"I don't suppose it makes much difference," Aunt Eva remarked, her eyes sparkling. "Married is married."

Overwhelmed by the confusion of emotion brought on by everything that had transpired in the last half hour, Beth fought the prickling tears that threatened. She wished then, more than any other time in her life, that her grandmother was alive. That would make the moment complete, she told herself ignoring the niggling thought that a certain, gray-eyed man would still be missing.

"Why not here with Reverend Thomas to officiate?" Beth said softly.

She left them arguing over who to invite and headed outdoors to greet the visitor. She frowned at the name emblazoned on the side of the truck and tried to remember where she'd heard it before. Winding Brook Ranch. Then she recalled that Ross had mentioned buying a mare from that ranch, located some twenty miles away over by St. Joseph. A portly man in sagging jeans and a shirt that was too tight over the belly stood at the rear of the two-horse trailer.

"There you are," he called when he spotted her. "I was just trying to decide whether to knock at the house or check one of the barns."

"What can I help you with?" Beth asked after introducing herself.

"Well, you could tell me where you want this filly?" he said, unlatching the rear door and swinging it open. A tiny set of spindly legs stamped and danced while the head tugged on the rope that tied her to the front of the trailer.

She was beautiful, even from this angle, all legs and soft red-gold fuzz with a feathery flag of a tail that flipped around like a flyswatter after flies.

"I'm sorry," Beth said. "I wish she was mine. Who were you looking for?"

The man's brow furrowed with confusion. "This is Thompson Farm, isn't it? That's what was on the mailbox."

"Yes, but—"

s the only one going out this week so
way I could've mixed things up. Let me
ow you the papers," he said, already opening the cab
door.

He pulled a sheaf of papers from a manila envelope
and held them out. "Tommy's Sunrise," he said. "Out
of Tommy Red. Damn good bloodlines, but then you'd
know that."

Beth didn't know, but she took the papers anyway
and thumbed through them. "There's some mistake,"
she insisted, "I didn't—" Her voice trailed away as
she came to the purchase contract with a photocopy of
a check stapled to it. And at the bottom was Justin's
signature.

"Damn," she muttered. "And double damn." The
check was dated the day after Brownie died. And this
bit of red-gold flightiness had cost him twice what he'd
paid for the fencing materials.

"Is there some problem, ma'am?"

She glanced at his concerned expression and forced
herself to smile. "No problem. Just a minute and I'll
get my foreman. He'll tell you what to do with her."

Beth forced herself to walk with apparent calm to the
house, and to even close the door gently behind her.
When she sagged back against it, though, all her poise
deserted her. Two tears trickled down her cheeks, and
great sobs threatened to escape. Why had he done it? It
was a wonderful, magnanimous gesture, but just now, it
felt like a cruel joke. Why hadn't he told her? Nobody
could just forget something like that.

"Charley?" she called.

Aunt Eva appeared in the living-room doorway
immediately, her smile changing to alarm at the sight of

her great-niece's pale, frozen expression. "Beth dea
what's wrong?"

Beth shook her head and covered her eyes. "Tell
Charley to handle things. I'm going upstairs. It seems
that Justin bought me a horse." She thrust the papers
she was still holding into Aunt Eva's hands.

"And that made you cry?" Charley asked from the
doorway, staring at her like every strange thing he'd
suspected about women had just been proven true.

"Everything's dated the day after Brownie died,"
Beth explained, then sniffed loudly as she struggled to
hold back the accumulation of unspent emotion.

"Oh, my" was all Aunt Eva could think to say.

"Saints preserve us from sentimental fools," Charley
muttered, and reached for the doorknob.

When he was gone, Aunt Eva pulled Beth into her
arms. She wasn't Grandma, but her warm embrace was
the closest thing to comfort Beth could think of.

"What are you going to do?" Aunt Eva asked.

Beth pulled back and wiped her sleeve across her
eyes. "I can't keep her. It's too much money. And it
hurts too much now to think about him. I don't need
any more reminders," she said, then turned toward the
stairway.

"Do you want me to call Justin?"

"Would you?" Beth felt like a coward then, but she
couldn't bear to talk to him just now. She'd already
sent the rest of his things to him, and he'd called Aunt
Eva to tell her they'd arrived. He hadn't even asked to
speak to Beth.

Only his Jeep remained, and it was parked out of
sight behind one of the sheds. Melanie was to pick it
up next month while en route to her parents' home in
Illinois. Beth had intended to be gone that day. Now,

ow. She couldn't think straight. Justin
was a greedy tramp, exactly what she'd
of her mother, no matter how much she still
ved the woman. And worst of all, it was all so
unnecessary.

As Beth lay on her bed, staring at the dancing shadows on the ceiling, she began to reevaluate her life. And she wasn't very happy with her conclusions.

Saturday dawned clear and cool, with a faint hint of a breeze that turned gusty by noon, blowing Beth's carefully groomed hair into its usual wild jumble of curls every time she stepped outdoors. As luck would have it, Edgar had remained out of sight all morning, so Beth hadn't been able to cage him. She only hoped he'd behave himself and not cause any trouble when the wedding guests arrived.

By one o'clock, the yard was full of dusty pickups and station wagons, and the house fairly bulged with well-wishers. The quiet, simple ceremony had swelled into the social event of the month.

As Beth bore dish after dish of food to the kitchen, she began to shed her melancholy. Not even she could be sad at such an occasion, not surrounded by so much gaiety and excitement. Even so, she had to wipe away a sentimental tear as she signed the marriage certificate on the witness line. It wasn't that she was sad or overly sentimental, she told herself. It was just hormones or stress, something like that. After she discreetly wiped her eyes, she dropped a kiss on Charley's cheek. The old man's startled, rheumy eyes misted, then he kissed her back.

"Wish your grandma could've been here for this," Aunt Eva whispered when it was her turn.

Beth smiled mistily. "She is. In here," she said, crossing her hands over her heart. Then before she could embarrass herself with full-fledged tears, she escaped to the kitchen and the cheerful chaos wrought by eleven women laying out a late buffet while they traded gossip and shared photos of grandchildren.

She was lifting the plastic wrap off a tray of petit fours when Aunt Eva called her to the phone. Squeezing her way through the shoulder-to-shoulder crowd, she picked up the receiver lying on the hall table. At first she couldn't hear above the din, so she stretched the cord into the bathroom. As she closed the door behind her, she recognized Justin's whiskey-rough voice in her ear. But the words were lost as a hundred small memories flashed through her mind.

"Beth? Is that you? Are you there?" The words finally registered.

"Why did you call?" she asked, her voice thin with shock. She wanted to talk to him, had picked up the phone a dozen times before losing her courage. But today, her emotions were too close to the surface.

"I had to congratulate my two favorite senior citizens," he replied.

"That doesn't explain why I just pried my way through a packed room to get to the phone."

His sigh was quite audible, and Beth half suspected he'd done it for effect. "I had to talk to you about the colt."

"Filly," she corrected automatically. "A colt's a male."

"Whatever. I want you to keep her."

"No."

"Why not?" Anger laced his tone now.

"Why did you buy her in the first place? And why didn't you tell me?"

He paused before explaining. "Brownie died, and you were so sad, so guilty. I wanted to find a horse that looked like her. Then I saw this one. I know it's the wrong color, but those big brown eyes simply enchanted me. I thought you wouldn't be able to resist her, not if you saw her."

But Beth had resisted. She hadn't allowed the filly's brown eyes or fuzzy coat of hair soften her. She couldn't afford to let anything crack her defensive shell, not yet. Later, she'd replace Brownie. When she was ready. When she could afford to. Maybe the horse wouldn't be from such blooded stock, but she'd buy it with her own money.

"I don't want her," Beth insisted.

"Your aunt told me you refused to have anything to do with the colt—umm, sorry—*filly*. She said you wouldn't even feed it, that Charley had to do it. Are you afraid?"

"Of a just-weaned horse?"

"You know what I mean," Justin said.

"I called the ranch," Beth continued, ignoring the issue at hand. "They refuse to take her back."

"Is that your answer to everything that scares you?" he asked in a taut voice. "Take it back? Send it back? Send me back? Hide in your tiny little corner of the world where you feel safe. Is all that familiarity and predictability really worth it?"

"I don't know," she whispered after a momentary silence. She was too confused by her own doubts, by the trembling that his voice aroused in her. Was her independence really that important? She feared this was one of those questions that couldn't be answered until she was old and gray. Choose now and let life decide whether she'd made a mistake.

"Keep the filly," he insisted. It wasn't a request or a plea, but an order spoken in a harsh tone that stirred the ashes of Beth's anger. That's all that kept Beth from surrendering to her weakness for him. And she had to resist him. She'd been wrong about Marlene's reason for marrying Alfred, but that hadn't changed the fact that the woman had nothing apart from her husband—no goals, no accomplishments, no sense of self. She'd crumple without him.

"You'll have to make other arrangements," Beth suggested. "Sell her. Or keep her. It's up to you," Beth insisted.

"Fine. Give me a week. I'll send someone for her," he said.

Before Beth could answer, the dial tone sounded in her ear. She realized she should be angry or maybe screaming with hysteria. But she simply felt detached, like she was hovering near the ceiling, watching her body go through the motions. Her mind and mouth seemed to work, conjuring up the right comebacks for the teasings of her neighbors. Still, a sense of unreality hung over her.

Slowly, Beth returned to the kitchen, her progress much hampered by the chattering crowd. As she squeezed through the doorway, it dawned on her that not one of the women in the room was within twenty years of Beth's age. Once it wouldn't have bothered her. Now she felt the difference acutely. It wasn't the years or the generation gap—it was the richness, the layered depths of their lives. Each had lived a hard but full life already and had another generation of loved ones to depend on and share with. When Charley and

Aunt Eva were gone, Beth would have nothing but vegetables and her pride.

Deciding to walk in the fresh air was the best way to ward off a renewed depression, Beth retrieved her old sneakers from the hall closet and slipped outside. No one seemed to notice her mismatched attire, or even that she was leaving. She felt an immediate sense of relief as she closed the door on the dull roar of voices and the overwarm closeness of the crowded rooms.

The wind gusted, stirring up dust devils and blowing her hair into wild disarray once again. She didn't care, though, now that the ceremony was over. The animals, she noticed as she reached the south pasture, were enjoying the brisk weather, all except Witch, who regarded the cavorting calves with a disdainful stare.

Then a wisp of red-gold appeared over the knoll, followed by a flash of black. The filly's hooves beat a wild tattoo on the ground as she raced over the top and down the slope toward the fence, with Edgar gliding along behind her.

Beth held her breath as Sunrise thundered full tilt up to the rusty wire, then sidestepped at the last instant and halted abruptly. Edgar swooped in and landed about fifteen feet away, then squawked loudly until the filly charged.

Beth watched them as they took turns chasing and retreating in a childish game of tag. She winced as the tiny, sharp hooves closed in on Edgar, but he always emerged unscathed. After a while, he tired of the game and landed on a leaning, half-rotted fencepost, cawing raucously. This time, when the filly charged, she misjudged and slammed into the post. She scrambled upright and snorted, then eyed the post with such bewilderment that Beth surprised herself by laughing. She was still smiling when she heard footsteps nearby and turned to see who was coming.

Ross Dixon stopped a few feet away and wiped his brow in mock relief. "I had to get out of there," he said. "That crowd of gray heads makes me feel like a snot-nosed kid. Charley even patted my head a while ago."

Another laugh bubbled up and Beth felt the tension inside her ease a bit more.

"That's better. You've been looking a bit grim lately," Ross commented as he leaned on the gate. "So that's the new filly."

Beth's smile faded. "Word gets around, doesn't it?"

"How's she doing? Halter-broken yet?"

Beth shrugged and began untwisting the wire that held the gate closed. "You'd have to ask Charley. He takes care of her. He's been in a bit of a daze lately, though. I can't think why else he'd put her out here. I'd better move her before she hurts herself or finds a hole in the fence."

"I thought Witch was the only one with that talent," Ross replied.

"I don't want to take any chances," she said. When she caught Ross's measuring glance, she frowned. "She's a valuable animal."

"I didn't say anything."

"No, but you were thinking it. I take it Charley's been talking," she said.

"A bit," Ross admitted. "He says you've been a grouch since you came back from California. Want to talk about it?"

Beth shrugged, refusing to take the bait. "Come on and help me catch her. Somehow I don't think she's going to just stand there and wait for me."

The filly didn't. However, they eventually succeeded in bribing her with a bucket of feed, and she followed them to the barn and trotted happily into a stall.

"She's beautiful, isn't she?" Ross murmured.

Beth straightened and brushed the dust from the sleeve of the silk dress. "Yeah, she is," Beth agreed in a soft, wistful voice.

Ross reached out and took Beth's hand, clasping it between his two warm, callused ones. "I'm told I'm a good listener." His eyes held a depth of understanding that startled her.

Beth shook her head. "Who do you talk to?"

"I could talk until my face turned blue, but it wouldn't change a thing for me," he said. "I just have to get on with my life. You know the cliché—change the things I can, accept those I can't."

"And somehow know which is which," she finished. "You seem to be doing a good job of it. What's your secret?" He was tanned and lean from hard hours of outdoor work. Although he still carried a hint of sadness, he wasn't melancholy or bitter. Just lonely.

He shrugged. "You'll have to find your own answers. Come on. My truck isn't blocked in," Ross said, slipping an arm around her waist and dragging her away. "Let's sneak away and get some pizza."

Beth drew in a ragged breath as she fell into step beside him. Maybe she could escape the memories and doubts for a while. "How about tacos?" she suggested. She'd never eaten tacos with Justin.

TWELVE

"Charley, the only thing wrong with this one is that he doesn't play poker. That's a poor reason for not hiring him," Beth stated, her patience wearing thin. She thumped the application form onto the desk and jammed her hands into her pockets to keep from throttling the cantankerous old man.

"He's just not right for the job," Charley insisted. He leaned back in the desk chair and propped his feet on an open drawer.

Beth glared. "Then who is?"

"Well, there's a young fellow out at the barn now," Charley said with a sly look. "He's waitin' for you. Just came out a while ago while you were still making deliveries. He might do." Charley's voice was casual, but Beth didn't miss the momentary gleam in his eyes. This one must know a bit about cards, she thought suspiciously.

"What's his name?" she asked, shuffling through the handful of applications as she spoke. The newspaper ad had yielded a smattering of phone calls and a few of the more serious applicants had made the drive out to the farm. But this one was the first to pass Charley's initial grilling. Beth's fingers stopped as she glanced over at the old man, who was rubbing his chin and muttering to himself.

Beth lifted her eyes to the ceiling and muttered a mild curse. "Does this guy have a name?"

"Carl something or other. Didn't fill out one of your papers. Nice boy. Your aunt said so, too."

"Did you tell him what the pay is?"

"He knows. Now get goin'. He's been waitin' a good while," Charley said with a not-too-gentle shove toward the door.

"Tyrant," Beth muttered. She didn't know whether to be grateful for the old man's apparent good humor or irritated at his interfering ways. But she still trusted his judgment.

Beth detoured through the kitchen and snatched up a freshly peeled carrot from Aunt Eva's salad fixings. Then she headed across the drive and through the gate along the path that led past the greenhouse, munching as she walked. At the barn, Charley had said, and she hadn't thought to ask why. Maybe the old man had already put this guy to work mucking out the stalls.

She was halfway there when she saw him. He moved like Justin, but Beth shook her head, more to dispel the thought than in denial. Justin was hundreds of miles away, in Nebraska, or maybe back in L.A. by now. But Charley's recruit looked a lot like Justin, which was reason enough not to hire him. It would be like working with a ghost.

Her feet slowed, then halted as she reached the fence. She stared at the man's lean figure as he backed out of the shadows into the bright sunlight. For a moment he stood still, murmuring to someone inside. No, not someone. Something. The red-gold filly dashed past him, then jerked around as she reached the end of her rope.

Then she set her feet, splaying her legs and bracing her hooves in the dirt. The man tugged on the reluctant filly's lead rope, moving with that catlike grace that seemed more animal than human. A heated awareness crept through Beth's body, followed by a tingling jolt of adrenaline as her mind accepted what instinct had already communicated.

Justin! She whispered his name, touching her fingers to her lips as the warring emotions tumulted through her. Why had he come? How dare he come and remind her how much she missed him, how lonely this farm was without him? Hope flared as her eyes drank in the sight of him, and she dared to think that she might have become more important than the glitz and glamour.

For the moment, he filled Beth's field of vision. His hair had grown longer still, curling over his collar. And he seemed leaner than she remembered. Then his startling blue eyes locked with her green ones. His grip slackened on the filly's lead rope.

Sunrise balked, then took advantage of Justin's inattention and jerked back. The rope slid through his fingers as he turned too late and reached into empty air.

"Come back here," he yelled, chasing after the trailing lead as the filly trotted toward the creek. He stomped on the dragging rope, then tumbled down the embankment into the rocky creekbed as the rope whipped out from beneath his shoe.

Beth leaped the fence the instant Justin disappeared over the creek bank. She reached him as he pushed himself to his feet and started brushing himself off.

"Are you all right?" she asked. Her voice was

slightly breathless, although she didn't know whether to blame it on the unexpected sprint through the field or the surge of fear she'd felt when Justin hit the ground.

"No, I can see that you're fine. No blood," she continued, babbling in her relief. Then, unforgivably, she started to giggle. "You looked so surprised."

"You think this is funny?"

She sobered some, but still couldn't suppress her happiness at seeing him again. "No. Yes. Well, it depends. You didn't bang your head on a rock or something," she said, reaching up to pick a weed from his hair.

He backed away before she could touch him. "I'll live. But that filly of yours is a problem," he growled out.

Stung, Beth blinked back the threatening tears. She wouldn't cry. She never cried. "She isn't mine," Beth answered. "I thought we settled that."

"You decided it," he replied. "But her papers still say she's yours." He turned his back on her without another word and started walking.

"Where do you think you're going?" She caught his shoulder, pulling him back around. For a panicked instant she thought he was leaving, walking out of her life again after turning her heart inside out one more time. She knew then that she wanted to explain, had to explain that she'd been wrong about Marlene, about everything, that she was miserable without him.

"I'm going to catch your horse," he ground out angrily. "Somebody has to teach her some manners. Since you haven't bothered, I guess it's up to me."

Beth glared. "I didn't ask you to buy her."

"No, you didn't. I don't blame you. You're busy and I suppose training a horse, even at this stage, takes a lot of work. At the time, though, I thought we'd be together, that we'd do this together," he said, stepping away from her.

"Justin?" she called tentatively as he turned away again. When he ignored her, she yelled louder. "Try a bucket of feed. Maybe you won't have to chase her."

He acknowledged her suggestion with a wave of his hand. "Why won't you listen to me, really listen, you idiot?" she shouted, then whirled around and stomped away when he ignored her.

She walked two laps around the lake before her temper simmered down enough to try talking to Justin again. She knew he hadn't left, because she'd taken the spark plug wires out of his Jeep. And if she knew Charley, the man would make it impossible for Justin to leave by any other means.

When she returned to the barn, she found Justin and Sunrise locked in another duel. Without a word, she took the rope from Justin's hands, allowing her fingers to linger only briefly on his.

"I think you both need a break," she said, dangling a freshly pulled carrot before Sunrise's nose. Ever curious, the filly's ears pricked forward, and she stretched toward it. Holding the carrot out of reach and gently tugging the rope, Beth crooned softly, copying Charley's singsong technique. She coaxed Sunrise into the barn, then flung the carrot into her stall. Sunrise trotted inside and munched greedily, barely noticing the gate that closed behind her.

"You forgot to unhook the lead rope," Justin reminded her as he stood behind her, watching the filly. Beth glanced over her shoulder, relieved to see that the anger had faded from his eyes.

"Nope. I meant to leave it on for a while," Beth

explained. "She'll step on it and get it tangled. Then she'll pull and find out it's better not to. She'll learn not to fight it after a couple of hours."

Justin frowned. "If it's that simple, why didn't you do it before?"

"I had my reasons. I guess I was too busy fighting my own rope, so to speak," she said, still guarding her feelings. He wore a wary expression as well, and she began to wonder if he was as unsure as she was. No, she decided in the next breath. Carl Justin Schnell, aka Justin Kyle, would never be unsure of himself with a woman.

"What were you trying to do, anyway?" she asked. *Why are you here?*

"I thought I was taking her for a walk. She looks so little and dainty, I had no idea she was so strong. Or so stubborn," he added with a pointed glance that made Beth's breath catch, although she tried to conceal how thoroughly his nearness was affecting her.

"She isn't a dog, for heaven's sake. You don't just put a leash on her and drag her along until she gets the idea."

"She acted like she'd never been touched," he said. "She kicked me when I tried to snap the rope onto her halter."

Beth winced at the thought of those sharp little hooves hammering into his satiny, tanned flesh. "How bad?" she asked.

"We'll still be able to have children, if that's what you mean."

Beth tried to laugh, to tell herself he was joking, that he wasn't making assumptions again. But his fingers brushed the nape of her neck, underscoring his meaning. She didn't know why he'd come, but she knew what he wanted at that moment. The trouble was, she found she wanted so much more. Before the sensual feelings could take hold, she pulled away from him.

"You don't give up, do you. There is no 'we' anymore. And you're not supposed to be here."

"You still care about me. I still care about you," he reasoned.

Beth turned and met his stare, baring her pain to him. "Yes, damn it. I still care. But nothing else has changed, either. You're only making things worse. So just stop."

"Why? Are you afraid you'll like it?"

Not wanting him to see the truth, Beth turned her head, staring over at the filly. "Why didn't you tell me you were coming to get her?"

"Two reasons. I figured you'd make sure I didn't see you. And I didn't know myself until the middle of the night when I was finally able to slip away from Greeno and a couple of others like him. I didn't want them to know about this place. It's probably the one peaceful corner left on earth."

Beth felt a twinge of guilt. "I'm sorry about Greeno. I guess Gull House isn't very private anymore."

"It's only a house," he said. "Besides, I've missed my room here, the creaking floors, the patter of rain on the roof, just knowing you're down the hall."

"You're not staying here tonight!"

"I still have a week left on my contract," he said.

"It's the middle of October. The contract was up two months ago."

He shook his head. "The contract was for twelve weeks. Not any specific date. I was only here eleven weeks before I had to leave. I'm back now, and I want to finish out the week. Anything after that is negotiable.''

"That can't be right." But she knew it was. She remembered the contract's wording clearly. She ought to, as many times as she'd made Aunt Eva read it the night Justin moved in.

"You're serious, aren't you?" she added, noting the implacable set of his chin.

He nodded. "Tony's a good agent. And I have a good lawyer."

"Just what are you implying?" Beth felt a shiver at the determined glint in his eyes.

"Breach of contract," he said, capturing her fidgeting hands. "I stay or you pay back the money."

"You know I can't."

He nodded. "So where do I start, boss?" he asked in a mocking tone.

He had her neatly boxed in and she knew it. She should have been angry, yet all she could think of was she'd been given a second chance. One week. It was enough time to convince him that she'd changed, that she'd learned that compromise was more rewarding than pride, that she'd based her decisions on all the wrong assumptions.

She might still have to say good-bye again and teach her heart to let go one more time. But they could make a lot of memories in a week. And maybe he would do something, say something that would make her angry, make her hate him, something that would make the good-bye easier. Or just the opposite. This good-bye could tear her into pieces. But she'd take the chance. She hadn't much choice if she wanted to stop the gnawing pain in her midsection.

"Come on up to the house, and we'll see what we

need to do to put Sunrise in your name," she said. She didn't expect him to agree, but maybe after a couple of days she'd convince him that actually she owed him. After all, she'd taken Gull House's privacy from him. But he surprised her.

"Fine," he said. "Let's go."

She glanced up, startled. "You agree? Why now?"

He leaned back against a stout beam. "I wouldn't want to entrust her to you. That filly is special. It'll take somebody special to bring out the best in her. I thought you had it, but obviously you don't."

Beth stiffened. "If that was supposed to hurt, thanks. It did."

"I didn't say it to hurt you. I did enough of that at Gull House, and I didn't believe a word of it, not then and not now. I came back to try one more time to make things work out. Maybe it was a mistake because you can't seem to see past the glitz and glitter to the real man. I'm Carl Justin Schnell. Justin Kyle is just a name in lights. He's whoever he has to be, whoever the director is looking for."

"I could see it," Beth said softly. "I always knew it. I just found it hard to believe, that's all."

"You're so caught up in this fantasy about independence and being different from your mother that you're blind to everything good we had. After all this time, I can't understand why."

"Grandma always said if it seems too good to be true, it probably is," Beth said, trying to explain. "She'd always been right before." Her hands quivered and she wrapped her arms across her chest, turning away from his angry glare.

"Yeah? Well, that works both ways," he retorted. "I thought I found a beautiful, sensitive woman who cared about the important things—the things that last. I thought I'd found somebody who wouldn't give a damn about whether I was on top or just a has-been. But I was wrong. You're just a scared little girl. And the hell of it is, I want you anyway. For a day, a week, whatever you'll give me.''

She whirled around and saw the unmasked vulnerability written across his face and walked straight into his arms. All her resolve, all her determination, was gone. And right now, she didn't care. His lips, his body felt too good against hers.

''I'm sorry,'' she said when he finally stopped kissing her long enough for her to speak. ''I've been an idiot.''

''So have I,'' he said. ''I should have known better than to go behind your back about anything. The timing was all wrong with Sunrise. That other time, I just wanted to help you out, to take away some of the worries. And forget what I said at Gull House. The thought of losing you hurt so much I just hit back the only way I could. I didn't mean to insult you.''

''It wasn't that, exactly,'' she said, struggling to find the words to express her fears. ''I've been afraid you'll swallow me up. I thought we'd have our time and then it would be over. I'd just be this shell that doesn't know how to be alone anymore. My mother was like that after Daddy left.''

He caressed her chin, then firmed his touch, forcing her to look at him. ''You aren't Marlene. And I don't think you see Marlene too clearly, either. She seems pretty tough under that show she puts on.''

Beth's brows pulled together in a deep frown. ''I talked to her. Rather, she talked to me. I thought she married Alfred for his money, but it seems I was wrong. But she still thinks that the only way a woman can have a good life is if a man provides it for her. I want to provide it for myself."

"You can," he said. "By the choices you make. Take a few risks. Marry me."

She chewed her lower lip while she studied him. He seemed pale and edgy, restless with uncertainty. He was a good man, as close to perfect as she could tolerate, and she'd be a fool if she threw away a second chance. Maybe she was stronger than she thought. Maybe it was only the strong who had enough courage to risk everything, to put their trust, their futures in the hands of another person.

Rising up onto her tiptoes, she touched her lips to his. "I can't promise to fit in with your friends or to be the perfect wife, but I love you too much to lose you again. If you want me, I'm yours," she declared.

"Every stubborn inch," he replied huskily as he pulled her against him and let his body tell her how much he wanted her. She slid her fingers from his shoulders down the length of him until he groaned and captured her hands.

"Later," he whispered. "We have a few things to settle first, such as how many children we'll have and when we'll have them."

Beth kissed him again. "Suddenly I'm feeling very maternal."

His voice roughened as he stroked gentle fingers down her back. "Funny, you don't look maternal. You look—"

"Willing?" Beth suggested, delighted with the smoky desire that sparked between them when she borrowed Charley's term.

"Among other things," he said, pulling her close. "I suppose you'll want to live here."

"I could adjust to California," she offered. "Maybe not the city, but someplace with some land. I hear there's a good market for organically grown vegetables."

"Your grandparents lived here and raised children here. So can we," Justin insisted.

Beth's eyes misted, and her throat tightened until she could barely speak. "We'd be stealing a few weeks together here and a weekend there. And don't even suggest giving up acting. You like it or you wouldn't have let Tony and Victor talk you into that second movie. You don't need the money that badly, do you? Because there's no great profit in farming. A good living at best, and you don't want to hear about the down side."

His smile widened. "I could buy a dozen farms and have money left over. But money doesn't mean much when there's no one to share it with. I'll share mine if you'll share your home, your life, your body, your thoughts, your children . . ." His voice trailed off as he nuzzled her neck.

"I'm glad you're as stubborn as I am," Beth whispered.

"Persistent," he corrected. "You're the stubborn one."

"Whatever. Let's go tell Charley. He's probably beside himself with curiosity."

Not surprisingly, the older couple were waiting expectantly on the porch, grinning broadly when Justin and Beth approached, walking hand in hand.

"Didn't know whether I'd have to get the shotgun to protect you, boy, but I see you handled her well enough," Charley commented. "When's the wedding?"

"Not soon enough," Justin replied, leading Beth into the house and toward the stairs.

"Justin, we can't," Beth said in a desperate, hissing voice. "Aunt Eva and Charley—"

"They're newlyweds," Justin said. "They understand."

"I don't think so," Beth said, even as she felt her objections melt under his touch. He paused on the landing to kiss her again.

"You mean this could be a shotgun wedding?" He sounded pleased. "Good. You couldn't back out."

"You can't think I would. I love you. And I want to marry you. It took a lot of convincing and a lot of thought. It took a long time for me to decide it could work—"

"Forever," he interrupted.

"That's why you can be sure this is what I want," Beth replied, eyeing him seriously, although it was hard to concentrate while his fingers stroked so seductively.

"Good," he replied, then stepped between her and the open stairwell, shielding her from eyes below as she felt the cool draft of air on her chest and realized her shirt had come undone.

"Thought me and Eva'd take a drive into town," Charley yelled up from the open front door. "Be gone an hour or two. Maybe three. What do you think?"

"Take all day," Justin called back, then lifted Beth over his shoulder and carried her the rest of the way to her room, oblivious to her laughing protests or to the front door slamming closed below them.